By N.R. Burnette
Copyright 2013 N.R. Burnette
www.nrburnette.com

Paper Edition

Special thanks:

I dedicate this to my mom and dad.
Sorry for the foul language, drugs, and prostitution in this book.
www.nrburnette.com

Cover art by Marina Shipova

By N.R. Burnette
]] half prologue [[

Thirty years ago, May 7, 2420

Daddy?

John's eyes popped open, head dizzy, his hands
jerked out. Was he falling? No, not falling. Zero gravity?
The date on his timepiece said it was two days later, its green
glow barely able to penetrate the pure darkness. John rubbed
his face, suppressing the emotions. He had heard his
daughter's voice again, and for a moment he had thought,
hoped, it was all a bad dream. That crippling, brief, moment
of hope...
No windows, no light, not even gravity. Just John,
floating in space in a cargo container, and the tiny visibility
that his timepiece could shed. He suffered the worst kind of
headache and thirst. He did not want to be alive. The
emotions came again, this time he couldn't stop them. His
sobs were quiet at first, but soon he was beating his head in
despair. His family dead, yet he was unable to join them.
He had lied to them about that.
Pity ran him over. He feared that he had days to
live. His breath was erratic. Days, when moments hurt like
an eternity. There would be no relief until he froze to death
or died of thirst, whichever came first. Unless he found a
way to do it, which reminded him, there was of course that
rifle. The rifle! He fumbled, shining his timepiece around.
"Where are you?!" John cursed, his voice weak. Using his
timepiece like a flashlight he spotted the energy rifle,
floating, its barrel misshapen from intense overheating. He
had put it through so much death, he really couldn't be
surprised that the barrel had melted. He snatched it anyways
and tested the trigger. A cold charge hummed for a lazy

second, but the rifle was otherwise ruined.

John began to sob. He had heard his daughter's tiny voice, when he was dreaming. Dreams filled with memories, nightmares. And then he heard her voice again, right now, and he wasn't dreaming. But he knew that was impossible, because his daughter was dead, and he had killed her.

]]Chapter 1[[

Present day, June 7, 2450

"Detective Taylor..." His reflection in the mirror grew more handsome each time he said it. Chestnut hair styled perfectly flat, his gaze balanced between want and disinterest, even his slacks held a confident crease. He looked like a man who could not be stopped.

Somehow his promotion shocked New Seattle City's finest, at least those hailing out of Precinct Four. It was no surprise to himself, of course. He twirled a pen on his desk, itching, craving, dying to see the faces of his fellow policemen. He left his office and smiled at his assistant, Catheri. She was as happy as he was. She would likely be the only one. "Back in a sec," he told Catheri as he walked by her desk. He wanted to see how his colleagues were taking the news. She glanced up and gently bit her lower lip, reminding Taylor that he had at least one person on his side. She was often on his side, or on his top, or on his desk, or wherever else. His office was behind her office, which afforded considerable privacy. He held the door handle for a savory moment before pushing it wide open.

Silence in the hallway of Precinct Four resonated like a bell, so much so that Taylor heard his lips part in a smile. Two uniforms were reading the announcement on the adjacent wall, one of them a very shocked Officer Grolsch. His application for the Detective position was a bit lacking, apparently. Grolsch had served over twelve honorable years and boasted impressive marksmanship, aptitude, and a high intelligence score. Grolsch would have made an excellent Detective.

Poor guy.

"How are you today, Officer Grolsch?" Taylor asked.

Grolsch said nothing. Taylor almost felt bad, Officer Grolsch looked so disappointed. Taylor heard someone mutter something about two years on the force, a voice he didn't recognize. Yes, Taylor had been an officer among them for only two years. They would get over it.

"Excuse me, everyone, there will be a celebration tonight for my promotion, and you're all invited," he said. A timed, automated scrubber whirred to life, the only sound made anywhere up and down the hallway.

This was too fun. Heads turned away, pretending to go back to what they were doing. Except Officer Grolsch. He had just spit on the floor while Taylor's head was turned. Maybe Officer Grolsch thought Taylor wouldn't see it, maybe he didn't care. But it was within an inch of Taylor's fine shoes, and he wasn't about to let that go unnoticed.

"Disgusting," Taylor said. He wanted to say, *you missed.* Grolsch just looked back at him. A couple heads cocked to see if there was going to be a little confrontation, and for a moment it was even quieter than before. Taylor waited, unflinching, until Grolsch walked away to a flood of whispers. Taylor was really going to enjoy this job. Having had his fun, Taylor walked back into Catheri's office and shut the door.

"That was fun. Where were we?" he asked Catheri, studying her blouse.

"Your wife called. She's on hold," Catheri said, blowing a tuft of crimson hair from her face.

"Take a message, tell her I've left for the day," Taylor said, his eyes still down her blouse. Maybe it was early, but leaving for the day sounded pretty good, actually. Taylor grabbed his black coat from the wood grain closet in his office as Catheri, Taylor's mistress, told Vina, Taylor's wife, yet another lie about him being gone. On a day like today, he wasn't going to deal with her. Today, he was on his time.

"Well?" he said, scooping an arm through his jacket.

"She wants to go to dinner…it's your two year

anniversary. Congratulations," Catheri said crossing her arms.

"Tonight? Really?" Taylor asked checking his wallet for cash. "Tell her something big came up, I'll be working all night."

Catheri took care of the call with a honey sweet voice, said goodbye, and set the phone down only to have it ring again.

"Detective Taylor's office. Yes sir, just one moment please," Catheri said. Taylor dropped his head.

"It's Keeb," she whispered. With a cross look Taylor snatched the phone from her.

"Detective Taylor speaking."

"Congratulations, my new Detective, are you ready for your first assignment?" Keeb asked in relative monotone.

"Boss, I was just about to celebrate," Taylor said still studying Catheri's blouse.

"I need you to report on a *323*. Meet me at Sethren Tower in fifteen minutes." Keeb ended the call. Asking if Taylor was ready was just a courtesy. People didn't say *no* to Keeb.

"Well, you heard the man, a 323. Something big *did* come up," he sighed. Fifteen minutes? The Commander was being generous. It should only take him five.

"It always does."

With a cocky step he hummed a beat out of the office, deflecting any scowls with a *screw you* smile. Through the visitor lobby he strolled, cutting across fellow cops, wincing at a handcuffed guy, and grimacing at a Citizen waiting in the lobby counter. Finally he pushed the tired double doors open and took a big breath of muggy July air, a New Seattle City blend. Blue sky, how nice.

Taylor bopped down the steps and stopped as a kid ran from his mom right in front of him, cutting him off. Adjusting his collar, he charted a course through the crowded sidewalk and began his strut. After passing mostly untouched through the crowd of degenerates, vendors, and bums, he caught a hearty whiff of coconut curry from the noodle cart on the corner of the street. Cutting across the street he found himself momentarily admiring the tightly wrapped curves of a blue haired punk girl. She quickly disappeared down the steps to one of the underground lightrail stations littering the city. Like the subways of old they boarded under street level and were the most efficient way to travel. Taylor continued on for a moment and then stopped. He *knew* that girl…

　　But how he knew her, he couldn't say. He spun around on his heels and jetted across the street where he saw the girl. Quick feet negotiated the steps down underground, which was always ten degrees hotter than street level. The lightrail station was like a city of its own with illegal vendors and abused glowing soda machines, a city where everyone faced the wall and waited for the train to come. Struggling to see around bobbing heads and a massive grey support beam, Taylor searched for a glimpse of that blue hair. He found her, waiting behind a sweating bald man for the Meridian route to arrive. Good, that gave him time to remember her. Taylor stayed relatively hidden behind other passengers waiting for his memory to kick in. He had fifteen whole minutes to meet Keeb, after all. The Meridian route was partly in the direction of Sethren Tower, he had until the 4th Street connection to end this intrigue.

　　The already petite girl just barely fit in her raven black body skirt and knee high boots. Her unnaturally blue hair fell perfectly straight. He noticed her eyes were framed with peacock feather tattoos.

　　Ayne. Her name is Ayne. *I forgot all about her*, Taylor mused. The eye tattoos were new. The Meridian route arrived and she hopped aboard, Taylor followed and snatched the seat across from her. He remembered now, a couple years ago he had responded to a call just weeks after joining the force. Whatever the details were she had basically assaulted her foster parents, which was a dangerous thing for an orphan to do. Taylor had leveraged that against her, made her rat out a few street contacts in exchange for a clean record. A girl in Ayne's position grew up hard and fast. He remembered physically cornering her during an interview once. He said something about how she needed to be a good girl and she reluctantly took off her shirt. She seemed both relieved and hurt when he laughed and made her put her shirt back on. She must have been fourteen then? Fifteen? As the transit departed, her eyes met his briefly.

Ayne forgot about me too. Taylor stood and crossed the cabin towards her, stepping gently as the A-Grav lifts jettisoned them towards the next stop. He sat next to Ayne, so close their shoulders touched.

"Hello Ayne."

She looked puzzled, until recognition changed her face. She mouthed a curse. Taylor checked his time. He was doing good on time so far.

"Still a cop?" she asked.

"Of course," he said. "Still misguided?"

"I got my own life now," she snapped. So much for submissive, she wasn't the old Ayne anymore. Taylor liked that, she had backbone. She held her purse *very* close.

"How is everything?" Taylor asked. She looked like her seat was on fire.

"Fine..."

It was awkwardly quiet for the next moment. Taylor wasn't sure where to go with this. He didn't even know why he was talking to her. He always liked Ayne, but clearly that relationship was one sided. He figured if that's how it was, then he was okay with that. Since they were talking, there was no point not messing with her. "What's in the purse?" Taylor asked. Taylor didn't really care, it was just the first thing that came to mind.

"Tampons," she said.

"Can I see?" Taylor asked.

"You got problems," she stood up and sat in another

seat.

Now Taylor *had* to have the purse. He stood up and walked over to her. "I could arrest you, then the purse is mine anyway," Taylor raised a half smile. "You don't have plans, do you? Nothing a couple hours of processing and sitting in a cell wouldn't interrupt?"

"What do you want?"

"I just want to see the purse," Taylor chimed.

Ayne looked in his eyes. "Then I can go?"

"Of course."

The lightrail stopped and the hatch slid opened, Ayne shoved the purse at Taylor and disappeared. Taylor watched Ayne run up the steps and disappear out of view. An elderly woman couldn't help but stare from across the train cabin. Taylor checked his time, they were near the end of Old Pike Place. The infamous Century Building was two blocks up, and Sethren Tower was on the other end of town. Taylor looked back at the old lady still staring at him.

"You want something, granny?" Taylor asked. The old woman shook her head and looked elsewhere. Anxiety grew as Taylor was getting close to being late. Looking up at the maps along the cabin ceiling he deciphered his route, snatching times, trains, and details with his short term memory. Within three stops and two trains later, Sethren Tower was in range. Taylor leaned back and opened his new purse, pleased with himself.

Inside Ayne's purse were zipkeys, a brush, spray, small picks, a cheap telecom, and a department store's inventory in makeup. Taylor found himself digging through them endlessly.

"Liar, there's not one tampon in here," Taylor said. His fingers stopped at a cold, familiar barrel housing. He peered in on a stocky, short Shibuya model blaster. Next to that was a tin case. He casually pulled the tin out and opened it to an illegal display of pills and powders. At least that was something. Taylor checked the time.

He was now a minute away from Sethren Tower, Pride of Sethren Company, Torch of New Seattle City, Major Cock Envy. It was the only skyscraper in the city less than a century in age. The previous newest was two hundred and seventy. Unlike most sky scrapers, Sethren Tower was not held together by moss and roots. Despite scarce resources and a comical price tag, it was built with all new materials. It was a beacon of the city, an icon of the mighty Sethren Company, pride of Jack Sethren himself... Now there was a guy who no doubt came from a long line of small dicks.

||Chapter 2||

Sethren Tower appeared in the midst of Taylor's day rant as the cabin rounded a corner.

Bleep. Bleep. It was Keeb calling. Taylor answered his telecom.

"How long are you going to make me wait?"

"I'm almost there sir. Hit a snag on the way over," Taylor had to be careful lying to Keeb. Keeb would remember everything.

The lightrail transit halted and fresh business suits spilled out as the doors opened. They herded themselves up the mezzanine to Sethren Tower. Taylor realized he was holding a purse full of illegal drugs and a blaster on his way to meet his boss, Commander Keeb. It seemed like a bad way to start his first day, like maybe that was more of a 'day two' sort of thing.

Taylor looked around for somewhere to stash the purse. Seven seating benches lined the mezzanine leading to the mouth of the tower. Sethren Tower didn't have doors on ground level, just an open mouth devouring all who entered. Taylor stashed the purse in a spot between a fern and a bench.

Shorter on time Taylor hustled up the mezzanine. He tried to look unimpressed as he strolled into the Tower lobby but his mouth could have dropped to the floor. Clean, shiny, polished floors and pillars of true granite, he had forgotten what *new* looked like. Pictures just didn't capture it. Taylor noticed the climate changed instantly, though there weren't any doors. That was a nice touch.

"Welcome, Detective Taylor, and congratulations on your promotion," a woman said. Taylor turned, wondering who could possibly know him here. He saw a receptionist, stunningly beautiful and poised behind an oval white counter. Her emerald eyes welcomed him from behind framed glasses, with matching green lips you could daydream in.

"Uh, thanks." He could say little more. Clearly, whoever designed this place sought to stun its visitors, leaving them soft and malleable for business negotiations. It did this first with its sheer size, then with its modern tech, and then with that smoking hot woman behind the desk. It was a man's tower.

"Commander Keeb is waiting for you on floor thirty seven," she said, suggesting the elevator doors behind her. Seven polished copper doors that all go up. If she knew there was a *323* up there, she didn't show it. She was perfect, too perfect. She met his awe with a smile.

"Do they treat you nice here?" he asked, resting his arm along the countertop. An elevator opened to a classic bell, Commander Keeb entered the lobby. His short gray hair matched the look burned into his face.

"You're late."

"What?" Taylor lied. He looked at his watch. He really was late.

"Follow me," Keeb said as he turned back to catch the elevator.

"So boss, about this three twenty--"

"Quiet," Keeb hushed him before Taylor could finish the sentence. They resumed their silent walk. *Surely they all know by now*, Taylor thought. And why was Keeb here in the first place? Sethren Company or not, it was just a dead body. Who gave a shit about that? It must be someone important, a political figure. What else would stir the Commander from his comfy chair? Keeb stepped onto the elevator, Taylor followed, trying not to give the impression of rushing. He hated being rushed.

The elevator doors shut. They gave a dark reflection on the inside, much darker than Taylor preferred. Keeb pressed a button. The floor numbers changed with dizzying speed as they transcended upward, and at floor thirty seven the elevator seamlessly stopped and opened. Taylor didn't have any fear of heights, but being this high up just felt different. He glanced down the hallway, which was poorly lit. Taylor couldn't shake the receptionist out of his head, as soon as he was done here he wanted to spend the rest of the day with her.

"Most of the lights on this floor are low to conserve energy," Keeb said. Taylor's head started to hurt. Really, why was Keeb here?

"Boss, any chance you could fill me in on some of the details here?" Taylor finally asked.

Commander Keeb stopped, turned to him with an unwelcome hand against Taylor's chest. Taylor didn't like being touched. "Sethren Tower is home to Jack Sethren, do you know who that is?" Keeb asked. It was a dumb question. Everyone knew of him.

"I've heard of him, sir," Taylor said.

"Everything about this investigation is confidential," Commander Keeb said.

"I got it," Taylor said.

"Good. We have a body and a witness. Talk to the witness first, we'll get to the body later," Keeb said. Taylor felt like he was being kept in the dark still, obviously there was more going on here. But, as a rule, Taylor didn't care too much about the details of his job. The less they want him to know, the quicker this will all take. He did, after all, have celebrating to do.

Sethren Company and Jack Sethren were modern day icons, leaders of the new world. He and his company practically pulled humanity out of the Darkening. Governors and billionaires brunched with Jack Sethren before laws were passed. Precinct Four suckled from a government breast, and he knew where the milk came from. So as a result, nothing bad ever happened here.

"This case will be handled exactly my way,

understand?"

"Sure," Taylor said, but again he was unsettled. Keeb wasn't a hand's on guy, never was. Something was putting pressure on him, and that was a thought that could make Taylor smile. The great Commander Keeb was under someone else's thumb?

They walked into the room where the witness was speaking to an officer. The room itself was plain, split in the center by a table, with chairs arching out of the base.

"That will be enough, Officer Spiel, thank you." Keeb dismissed him. The officer left, shaking his head. The witness rambled on, oblivious to Officer Spiel's departure or Taylor's arrival.

"...and that's when I killed him," the man sobbed.

Taylor looked at Keeb. "Case closed, Chief."

"There's more to it than that," Keeb said. He pulled the chair next to the man and sat by him, placing a hand on his shoulder. "Tell Detective Taylor what you told Officer Spiel, just one more time."

"I already told you!!" The table jumped from his fists.

"Just one more time," Keeb said gently. "The Detective needs to hear this. It will help us find the guy," Keeb said. Taylor was confused. Find who? Wasn't that a confession? Wasn't Taylor just here to maintain appearances? Keeb had a suspect, he was certain of it. Taylor wouldn't actually have to investigate anything. The witness contemplated Keeb before he stood and turned his back to them. He wrung his hands like a wet towel, forcing himself to recount what happened.

"He gave me a choice. Kill my son, or watch him suffer."

Taylor blinked. What did he just say? Taylor was suddenly tuning in to the details of this man's story. Did he kill his own son? Or rather, was he forced to kill his son? Taylor thought about that for a moment. Nope, he hadn't heard that one before.

]]Chapter 3[[

Taylor took a longer look at the man. His name was
Kayd Lad. His fingers were stained with blood, hands limp
on the table. They were not a workman's hands, Taylor was
sure. They showed the soft skin of wealth. The man never
took his eyes away from them as he recounted what
happened. Taylor and Commander Keeb sat across the table,
listening amidst weeping and sobbing. Taylor did his best to
look concerned. Strangely, for all the trappings of wealth,
Kayd carried an impressive neck scar.

"You never escape your past," Kayd said. His face
changed upon saying it.

"What?" Taylor asked.

"…after all this time," Kayd said. Keeb and Taylor
looked at one another.

"That's enough Kayd," Keeb said, "…we have
everything we need. Taylor?"

"Nothing more." But Taylor did want more. Kayd
was about to reveal something curiously arousing.

Keeb motioned to leave. Taylor stood, curious about
what Kayd might say next. For Taylor, curiosity was the
only thing about his job that he enjoyed. He could care less
about words like *victim* or *justice*. He preferred words like
recognition and *paycheck*. Keeb wasn't going to satisfy
Taylor's curiosity though, they still had a body to look at and
nobody wanted to be here all day. Another body, Taylor
hoped the eyes would be closed. He hated when they were
open, open eyes always haunted him for a day or so. He had
to admit the idea of catching this killer almost stirred him, if
nothing else it was a little different. High profile cases
meant a bit of fame as well. But first things first.

Keeb turned to Taylor in the hallway once the doors
slid shut behind them. Taylor looked up at him, hoping for
some insight into why he stopped Kayd short.

"The body is in room V over here, CSD has already

documented the scene. Just take a look and make sure Kayd's story matches up," Keeb said.

"That's five, sir. Old Roman numerals for five, not V," Taylor corrected him. He wished he hadn't. Keeb's expression darkened in a way that said Taylor should forever keep his mouth shut.

"Just take a look, Detective," Keeb said softly, though with no lack of intensity, and left for the elevator.

Room five, with a V. Taylor hadn't seen a dead body in days.

The room was cold. The body lay face up, sprawled atop the center table. Two glossy eyes stared out. *Dammit.* His name was Jack Lad, and he was Kayd's oldest son. His left hand was mangled, the attacker's way of convincing Kayd to euthanize him. The hand was so disturbing Taylor had to look elsewhere. Seeing the body suddenly made Kayd's story real.

The body showed a stab wound in the chest and abrasions on the neck. Blood covered the table like a red sheet. The weapon, a bayonet, stood point first on the table. Analysis should confirm Kayd's prints.

Where to begin? Taylor surveyed the room, though he didn't really know what to do. Suddenly he was reenacting every detective story he ever heard. He was almost tingly. There was the body for starters, he should look at that for a minute. If someone was watching him, he wanted to look the part of Detective. Appearances were everything. After walking around the body in an analyzing way, he then looked under the table. Nothing there of course, but it seemed like a good idea visually. He thought about looking under the body a little, lifting the hands to check the fingernails and such, but he didn't really want to touch it. *Surveillance*, he thought. Taylor inspected the ceiling, walked along the walls, dipped his head under the table. He even looked behind paintings for anything that looked like a camera. Tech with micro cameras could be all over this place, but he wasn't finding any. He *could* ask security about any cameras, but Keeb probably wouldn't like that. He didn't want Taylor to venture out beyond what he had already given him. Then again, Commander Keeb had already left.

Taylor craned his head outside Room V, and scanned the dim hallway for anything that looked like surveillance. Unless a long carpet runner and the occasional potted plant were on the list, he was still empty handed. With his eyes down the hallway he saw the victim, of sorts, Kayd Lad cross the floor to another room. Taylor was surprised to see him still in the building.

There was a gun in his hand.

"Kayd? Mr. Lad?" Taylor called out. Where were the officers who had been talking to him earlier? The door to their conference room was open, they had already left. Kayd must have gotten up and retrieved the gun the moment he was left alone, Taylor just caught a glimpse of him before he disappeared into another room. He wouldn't answer Taylor's calls, and the door wouldn't open. With his ear against the door, Taylor heard muffled crying.

"Come on Kayd," Taylor pounded on the door. *BANG*!

He flinched at the unmistakable sound. Taylor stepped away from the door, slow and still. He remained motionless except for his heart beating, which filled the hallway. He felt the tower swaying ever so slightly. Tall buildings did that.

"Kayd?" Taylor said.

Taylor stood, dumbfounded. Should he break in? Well, no. Either Kayd was dead, or he had just shot a potted plant to relieve stress. Either way, it had nothing to do with Taylor, except possibly a long night of paperwork. If Kayd just shot himself, and someone found him later, Taylor would be off shift and wouldn't have to deal with it. Besides, what really happened? *Nothing*. He wasn't sure if he even saw a gun in Kayd's hand. And that sound could have been anything, or so he tried to convince himself. Taylor had important plans to celebrate. Besides, suicide was a personal choice. Kayd couldn't live with what he did. So what?

Screw it, what do I care? Taylor clenched his teeth. *Bleep. Bleep.* Keeb was calling on the telecom. Taylor hoped he didn't already know somehow.

"Detective Taylor speaking."

"Taylor. I forgot to say, I need your report by nine tomorrow morning," Keeb said.

"Fine." Taylor looked at the door. *Forget it.* Nine a.m.? Taylor hated early mornings. He looked one last time at the door, ignoring any kind of obligation. He really could just walk away. The thought consumed him all the way down to the lobby floor. He saw the receptionist again, just as beautiful, though he didn't smile at her this time. Her crimson hair matched her eyes and lips. He swore they were green earlier.

He felt awkward leaving like this, like he was stealing something. He wanted to tell someone. His headache pounded. The city coroner walked by on his way to remove young Jack Lad's body. Taylor just nodded at him. Maybe the coroner would be picking up Kayd's body too, you know, father and son thing. Taylor grimaced, that sound could have been anything, and it didn't matter either way. He had a promotion to celebrate.

When he boarded the lightrail transit, having been judged under the darkening sky, he sat and watched the doors close before he remembered something. His hand slapped against the plexi-screen in protest.

"Shit!" From inside the lightrail cabin he watched the bench where he stashed Ayne's purse.

7 p.m.

Catheri had given up waiting for Taylor to return to the office. If she waited any longer she wouldn't make it home on time. Maybe he'll still visit her tonight. He did say something about celebrating. Catheri hustled her things together and closed the door. She planned the evening as she exited the lonely hallway. Her house was a mess, and she wasn't sure if her son Jaek had eaten or not. She would need to cook dinner, tidy the bedroom, take a quick shower, shave her legs, re-apply makeup, and conceal the perfect lingerie. She had a full schedule. If only Taylor would tell her *when* he was coming over it would be so much easier. She had waited more than once outside his house or his transit stop to surprise him with something quick and naughty, just to be left waiting naked underneath her long jacket. She stopped trying to be spontaneous after that, especially when a very drunk man noticed her lack of clothing and tried to follow her home.

The evening sky had begun its dark descent, casting shadows as she hurried to the transit station. The late duty officer who had just started waved as he walked his perimeter of the YARD, a vehicle depot, housed across the street from the precinct. Catheri's feet always ached on the last two steps of the stairs and it always took about five or six steps to get used to the concrete on the sidewalk. A man in a business suit stopped and turned as she walked by, trying to get a look at her. She was used to that. The noodle cart on the corner smelled amazing, but she couldn't eat from someone whose forehead was as shiny as the food.

The transit station still bustled, it would be just as busy all night. The Citizens here never slept. A line of people, all men, waited. Catheri dug into her jacket pocket, removed her Samsung gt4 shades from her purse and half watched a show as she waited for the next lightrail. The shades kept men from trying to talk to her, while giving them the opportunity to look.

Catheri couldn't stop agonizing over her plans tonight if Taylor came over. She remembered a time when men didn't affect her like this. Jaek's dad certainly never did. It was different with Taylor though, they were in love. Even though he was married, he really loved *her*. But it was complicated. Things were always complicated with married men. Her mother warned her of that. She was a single mother now, and that was a depressing thought for a woman. Most men, especially someone as important as a Detective, would avoid any serious commitment to a woman with a child. Being widowed was her saving grace, because despite a degenerate society, single moms were frowned upon.

Anymore Taylor seemed distracted, but he was a new Detective now. He was probably just stressed out, making sure he did a good job on his first day as Detective to impress the Commander. His mind was in two places at once. She could help him refocus, she just needed to be a little sexier and more understanding.

In the corner of her Samsung shades a bleep indicated someone calling her. *Taylor*! She brought her hand to her ear to cup the tiny speakers in the shades.

"Hello?" she asked innocently.

"What's a beautiful woman like you doing on a night like tonight?"

She smiled. "Waiting for you to call."

"Good, I need you to do me a favor," Taylor said.

"Lost your wallet again?" she joked, masking apprehension. His favors never went well for her.

"I'm following some leads, and I need you to pick something up. Go to Sethren Tower, and just off the lightrail stop go to the farthest bench to your right. Grab the purse that's hiding there and take it home, I'll meet you there later," he said.

Yes! Taylor was coming over tonight. A mess of plans involving dinner, candles, and the right outfit flittered through her mind. "Sethren Tower? ...okay, Taylor, I love you." Catheri bit her lip. By the time she went to Sethren Tower and got home, Jaek would be in bed. She hadn't seen him all day. Taylor hung up without another word. At least he was coming over tonight.

Catheri frowned as her usual stop came and went, consoling herself patiently until the route took her to a different union station. She boarded the lightrail that stopped at the Tower on the other side of town. She had been to Sethren Tower once, while it was being constructed. It was an embarrassing memory actually. After a night of drinking with her girlfriends they all got the urge to run naked in front of the Tower. They were surprised to find the night shift construction workers there, all burly men admiring the show. *Ahh, the good old days.*

A college student, judging by his wrinkled clothing, kept trying to make eye contact with her. She gazed out the plexi window. From a distance Sethren Tower imposed, pinned against the horizon. They approached their stop.

Catheri was seeing the finished Tower up close for the first time but didn't have time to stare in awe. As the lightrail dropped her off, she hurried over to the bench Taylor had described and found a purse hiding there, just like he said. Taylor had never asked her to do anything like this before, it must be something important.

Two mid-twenties men in business slacks and one finely dressed woman conversed thirty meters away, and none seemed to notice her. She stooped down casually and picked up the purse as if it were her own. Which was ridiculous, it didn't match her outfit at all.

The stop at Sethren Tower was above ground, one of the few stops that didn't occur down a flight of steps. Catheri looked inside the purse, digging through brushes and makeup, until her fingers felt something that stilled her breath. Cold, metallic, cylindrical. A blaster? Her hand jerked back as if stuck by a needle. Catheri hated this sort of thing. She knew Taylor would protect her, but it still felt illegal. She jumped when footsteps sounded, then a man stood next to her. He was also waiting for the lightrail, though paranoia made her wonder. She regretted taking off her shades, wishing she could hide behind them. She didn't dare reach for them now, she was too nervous to do it without her hands shaking. Why did she get so nervous so quickly?

"Nice night," he said. He looked middle thirties, like her. A warm genuine smile, dark hair, pressed slacks and a business coat. Successful and handsome. She looked at him as casually as possible, too terrified to speak. Any second her nerves would give her away. Breathe. Be calm. There's nothing in the purse. Nothing in the purse. Why was he looking at her? He did have very nice eyes.

"I said, nice night out, isn't it," he tried again. Catheri was used to men wanting to talk to her. She spent hours a day in the mirror making sure of it.

"Maybe..." she returned, struggling a smile.

Maybe?! Why on EARTH did I say that? She clutched the purse like it was trying to spill itself all over the floor. He was unfortunately good looking, but a little uncertainty was in his gaze now. She gave him another smile, trying to defuse the awkwardness, and opened her mouth as if to say something, which left her mouth half contorted. Then, she couldn't think of anything to say, so she looked away. That had to be the worst smile ever. The purse was being crushed underneath her death-hold. Great, now this great looking man thought she was crazy, he even took a safe step away from her and cleared his throat. The silence was almost painful, broken only by the train that couldn't come soon enough. What was wrong with her? Catheri practically leapt onboard and buried herself in the corner, hiding the purse between her and the wall. The man still wore a quizzical expression as he boarded, sitting comfortably far away from Catheri.

She knew what was wrong with her, it was the *instant guilty conscience syndrome*. Catheri prided herself on the ability to exude 'out of your league bitch', except for when she was hiding something. She scratched, fidgeted, fixed her hair. She checked the time on her wrist and still didn't know what time it was. She tapped her foot, waiting for the next changeover station four minutes south down Franklin Ave. She checked the time again, almost eight p.m. Jaek would be crawling into bed soon, by himself. She didn't even see him today. She reached for her shades and called home, Jaek answered on the third ring.

"Mom"

"Hi honey, I had to work late tonight. Did you--"

"I ate. Brushed my teeth. Going to bed."

"Right. Okay. Well, I'll be home soon to tuck you in to bed," she said.

"Whatever," Jaek hung up. Fifteen year olds were so short on the phone sometimes.

At least he'll be asleep when Taylor comes over. I can wear something silky.

||Chapter 4||

"It's a murder case, Vina," Taylor said to his wife.
"I can't discuss the details. You understand." One of the
benefits to being a cop was that important case at odd hours
of the night. His marriage depended on it. He pulled the
phone away while she recited what he expected her to say.

"But tonight's our second anniversary! Taylor...we
haven't been husband and wife for…well, it isn't proper to
talk about such things, but, it has been awhile. I feel like I
never see you," Taylor watched from inside the transport as
Catheri's stop came into view. Lower Renton had seen a
decline from its previous glory, but it was still a grade above
Mt Lake or Old Capitol Hill.

Taylor walked the three blocks from the transit stop
to Catheri's house. Precinct policy restricted interoffice
affairs, not that he gave a shit. No one would recognize him,
and even if they did he was a Detective now. Detectives
often had business that never needed explanation. Taylor
tuned back to Vina's voice on the phone.

"Look, I need to make a good impression with this
first case," he told her. "I have to go, I'm about to talk to a
witness," he said.

"I love you," Vina said before Taylor hung up.
Taylor gave that a moment to think about it, for some reason
she sounded different that time. He always hung up like
that, but her voice was different. Was she getting sick of
him finally?

Taylor rounded the corner, brushing against a rusty
chain fence. The wind was always amplified on this block,
unless it was his imagination. Maybe it was the slanted
roofs or the exact twelve meters between each house,
funneling air. Taylor walked down the uneven sidewalk as
small droplets of rain pecked at him. He judged the rain

would disperse into a moist fog by midnight. Residents of New Seattle City were experts on predicting rain.

Catheri's house was west on Lakeview Street. He never understood how a widowed mom afforded to live here, it was almost middle class. The walk was brief and the night air was crisp. Taylor managed the concrete sidewalk and walkway to her front door, admiring her hourglass lawn and the hedging that framed it. Fresh grass was the best part of Renton, and he oddly appreciated it, even though it tended to overrun the sidewalks. He finally climbed the porch steps and stopped at her door for a moment. He placed his hand on the beige wooden door and pushed it open.

Stepping inside Catheri's house he first noticed the dimmed lights and scents of vanilla and cinnamon. Candles. He didn't give a care for them, but he knew it meant Catheri wanted to have a special night. Taylor was good at picking up cues from other people, women especially. Her son Jaek was probably asleep, Taylor was glad about that. He hated dealing with that little punk. Catheri was slicing a baguette in the kitchen when he walked in. Her main living room was surrounded with dark blue walls. Goblets of red wine were set on the table, candles flickered from the draft of the open door, and Catheri wore a silk gown that was trying to slip off. It looked new, black with sparkling embroidery, transparent in all the right places. Being his second anniversary with Vina, he felt a little guilt. He hadn't felt that in a very long time. Strange.

"Well hello, *Mr. Detective*," she savored as he stepped inside closing the door.

"Did you get what I asked for?"

"I've been waiting for you," she came over and wrapped her arms around him gazing up into his eyes.

"Where is it?" Taylor asked.

"Can't it wait?" she toyed with his collar.

"No"

Catheri rolled her eyes and marched into the kitchen, returned with Ayne's purse and thrust it at him. "Here." She walked back into the kitchen and sliced more baguette pieces. Taylor examined it briefly. *Good.* Taylor tossed the purse aside and wrapped his arms around Catheri's waist, burying himself against her.

"Now, what were you saying about me?"

Some would feel lucky to be in close contact to Jack Sethren, *THE* Jack Sethren, savior of New Seattle City, its most powerful and most prominent Citizen, the man who made '*Jack*' the top baby name, but Commander Keeb knew better. He hated every minute of it.

"Is that going to be a problem, Herald?" Jack Sethren said over the phone. Yet another request, another cryptic instruction, and for whatever reason, it usually had to do with Taylor.

"No, Mr. Sethren. I assure you, I have Taylor under control," Keeb said.

"Good, Herald. I can always count on you."

Commander Herald Keeb hoped he didn't have to reply to that. Luckily, Jack Sethren ended the call first. Keeb dropped the telepiece and held his head, staring at his desk. He could hear the soft, rhythmic snores of his wife in the next room. He hated dealing with Jack Sethren, a necessary evil in today's world he supposed. To think, people actually loved him.

Jack Sethren was playing a game with Taylor, and whatever it was about, Keeb didn't want to be part of it. Unfortunately, he didn't have a choice. He toyed with the file he had on his desk, Taylor's new murder suspect. The name in the file wasn't part of Jack Sethren's plan, but Keeb had his own personal vendettas to resolve. Whatever Jack

Sethren thought, Keeb was not a puppet. Tomorrow evening there would be an arrest. Jack Sethren could keep being wealthy scum, and Keeb could keep being less-wealthy scum. All in a day's work. Whatever his peculiar interest in Taylor was, Keeb didn't care.

Keeb undressed on his way to the bedroom and carefully slid into bed between cotton sheets. His wife rolled over and draped an arm on him. He pulled away and stared at the wall. He was not a puppet.

Taylor dumped the purse out on the street corner, scanning each falling hairbrush, lipstick, and eyeliner to make sure he missed nothing. The blaster was gone. He slammed the purse to the ground and stomped on it.

"Damn it!"

Catheri wouldn't dare take it, she would sooner turn herself in for a crime she didn't commit than do something like that to Taylor, but he had an idea who did. Her punk son Jaek, that awkward teenager full of anger and resentment, he must have snooped through Ayne's purse and found the blaster. What the hell did Jaek need a blaster for? Stupid kid. Taylor wanted to turn around and go back for it, but aside from the insult of having something stolen, Taylor didn't really need it himself. He always stashed a couple of unregistered blasters that couldn't be linked to him, just in case he needed someone dead. Only idiots would use their own service weapons. Jaek would hopefully just shoot himself with it anyway.

"Screw it. I'm finally a free man tonight," Taylor whistled to himself. It was late into the night and he was long overdue for a little fun. Thankfully it shouldn't take him more than fifteen minutes to get downtown. He still couldn't shake his thoughts, that stupid kid Jaek really pissed him off. But the closer he came to the heart of degeneracy, that is, New Seattle City's night life, the more he was able to forget about it. Taylor examined the collection of drugs he stole from Ayne and grabbed one that looked like a Red Hat. He didn't want to worry about Keeb. In fact he wasn't going to worry about anything. He popped it and another one after it. It was finally time to celebrate. His throat and tongue were already feeling tingly. He had waited *all* day for this. He closed his eyes for just a second—and when he opened them he felt a ball of energy forming in his feet. It moved up his leg, into his stomach, and up across his arm, following wherever he looked. He felt like he was controlling it, moving it, shaping the ball. Taylor rested his head on the seat and felt the effects of the Red Hat grow and fill him completely. This was going to be good.

Hours later, he was bopping down the street. A clown was following him. He knew there wasn't a clown, and that this was a hallucination from the drug, but this clown was a fucker. And damn it, he was a funny one too.

The late night food vendors and neon lights of downtown blurred together, reforming wherever he turned his head. He didn't remember getting off the lightrail, but the first thing he was aware of was him staring at a tree near the college district. Taylor began to skip and he thought of Ayne. Why he thought of her he didn't really know. But he was hoping to see her again.

Halfway through making love to Catheri he realized he was going to track down Ayne. Not that Ayne was so special. His mind often wandered when making love. Some excitement was there at first, usually, but sex eventually bored him. Looking into Catheri's eyes was uncomfortable. She would look at him with eyes so full of love that he had to look away. He spared her feelings as much as he could, and in bed that meant burying her face in a pillow more often than not. Avoiding eye contact was the trick. She would do anything for him, and *that* was all he really wanted.

Taylor felt the old, wise skyscrapers staring down at him, judging and smiling with their glowing windows for teeth. When Taylor looked over his shoulder, he saw the clown following him still. Its eyes never left Taylor. Taylor glared at it with an intimidating look, which he shouldn't have. Taylor couldn't stop laughing now, walking backwards and trying to stay on his feet as he went from sidewalk to curb. He bumped through a couple, almost knocking over a girl wearing brown tights and a black skirt. They were watching a juggling act, and Taylor found himself suddenly surrounded by swirling neon lights from the twirling electric balls. Angry shouts burst from the rest of the crowd, but Taylor's eyes were fixated, otherwise he would have flashed his badge and put them all in their place. It felt as if the swirling lights of this juggling act were rewiring his brain. He heard his heartbeat, listened as it slowed, and panicked as it stopped. Did it really stop? No, that was just his high playing with him. He really didn't want to start freaking out. Taylor walked away from the swirling lights, standing in the middle of the street. Three men in furry jackets, perhaps they thought it was wintertime, were huddled on the corner. One of the men looked away from him, he did it in a way that meant he was being watched. Idiots. They couldn't take him, let them try!

"HEY!" Taylor yelled at the three men. "HEY!" he yelled again.

The one who had been looking at Taylor looked to the man on his left, which told Taylor who the leader of this trio was, and with a curt shake of the head the three of them started walking away. They had likely intended to rob him, picking out a well dressed man who was blazed and drugged beyond belief, they had thought they spotted an easy target. Taylor was going to show them, he started to follow. Little bitches, three against one, and who was running scared? Not Taylor.

Ayne's old street corner was nearby.

What a shitty first day! He stumbled a moment when gravity played a trick on him. He tripped, hustling past blasting music from a nightclub, the sounds were too loud to know where his head began and the music ended. Taylor didn't want to lose those three guys, he had a lesson he was going to teach them, but when he looked up they were gone. Instead he had stopped in front of a Neo Kobe gift shop. In the doorway of the gift shop he heard familiar groaning, a greasy haired man someone smothered against the wall, drilling his body into her. By the look her bare knees poking through tattered stockings, she spent as much time there as she did against the wall. This late at night a prostitute could be taken in the doorway of a gift shop. Taylor hid his badge. This late at night, nowhere was safe, not even the steps to Precinct Four. He wasn't sure if he hid his badge to discourage attention, or to encourage it, or he just needed reassurance by touching it. The fact that he was thinking of his actions meant his raucous high might be coming down.

Old Pike Place market inspired and entertained the dark minded wanderer after dusk, a world apart from New Seattle City. Forever near the harbor and reeking of fish, it was a street length mini market that went three levels underground. During the day there were painters, musicians, dealers, gamblers, a pachinko arcade, and a small zoo. At night, you didn't want to go down there except to look through the windows of the zoo. Taylor remembered one night he sat staring into the eyes of a Russian turtle at three in the morning. It gave him a new level of perspective, or at least he imagined it could. Taylor watched two shadowy men emerge from the west entrance to Pike's Place Market, they walked with a sort of adrenaline mixed with anger. Taylor knew, he just knew, that he could walk down there right now and find someone bleeding out on the floor. And he knew that if he did, someone would be waiting for Taylor to leave so they could sift through the pockets of this dying person. Taylor didn't care, no one died down there who didn't deserve to die.

An amber eyed girl motioned at him. The clown came back, he was behind her, thrusting his hips. Taylor couldn't help but smile, that clown was too funny! Taylor didn't want a screw, but she saw him smile and so she came over, draping her arm from his neck to his chest like a silk tie.

Her perfume sent Taylor into another high. Her breath warmed his neck, lips glistening like a purple lolly pop. She had a hook shaped scar on her left cheek, and her hair slithered with snake implants. Taylor liked those, they nudged his chin as she leaned in close. It made it feel like he was with Medusa. Or maybe it was all just the Red Hat talking.

"You lonely tonight?" she asked.

Taylor showed her some cash but pocketed it deftly before she could snatch it. She got down on her hands and knees like a cat, Taylor leaned against a gift shop window. That was his favorite part of oral sex, watching a woman go to her knees. After that it didn't feel like much, at least not to him. He felt her tug on his pants, Taylor glanced up at the sky. His belt and top button were undone so easily it would put Catheri to shame, women usually struggled with the top button more. Not this girl, she was a pro. He relaxed and studied the dark clouds high above him. Cold air hit his legs as his pants came down, then a warm, moist feeling hit another part of him. Somewhere behind those clouds was a universe of stars, spaceships, colonies, and who knew what else. He lit up a smoke and forgot about Ayne, about Kayd, about his report tomorrow, about his anniversary. *I should bring home a gift. Flowers. Vin would like those. I should do something nice, I'm always an asshole to her.* He opened his eyes. What was wrong with him? Now he felt guilty? Taylor didn't feel guilt. He had no reason to.

     "Damn it," Taylor said, pushing the girl aside and wandering off into the street. He toppled a garbage can over and spilled its contents across the street, claiming the attention of anyone within earshot. Taylor headed for nowhere in particular but down an alley, where he went about thrashing another garbage can. Later he remembered crawling next to a recycling bin, sitting down, and mildly hoping his kidneys were still in his body when he woke up. *If* he woke up. He didn't really care if he didn't.

]|Chapter 5|[

John's story did not end in that cargo container, floating through space. Though in truth, it should have. But, a twisted fortune smiled just once upon a dying man who was forced to kill his own wife, son, and daughter. His vengeance was given a gift, a chance, a way to make the bastards who did this suffer, as he suffered. It would not bring his children back, nor could it in any way save John, because in fact, John was already dead.

He just didn't know it yet.

John was going to kill the men responsible, or rather, force them to feel what he felt, force them to kill their loved ones. But he couldn't remember more than that, not really, and when he tried to remember, he blacked out. His parameters weren't designed to handle complex algorithms like that, apparently, and a software reboot was usually required. So, he learned not to think of those things if he could help it, and he waited. John had waited, he had waited for so very long. Finally he found one of them, Kayd Lad, and at long last he tasted the first course of his revenge. Kayd had suffered deeply, and Phonm was next. The lights were off in Phonm's house, but John could see just fine. He was waiting there, waiting in a closet for Phonm to come home. John could wait forever if he needed to.

"Daddy, how long do we have to wait in here?" she said. John was glad he didn't have to wait alone. His daughter was so beautiful. She had stayed by his side, forgiven him for what he did to her, for killing her. She understood how hard it was, but how necessary it was too, and she even helped John find the bastards responsible. Her death was a painless one, at least for her.

"Not much longer sweetheart," John said. His little girl crossed her arms, tired of waiting so long in the dark for Phonm. Phonm's wife, Ellen, finally came home. That was good. She was going to be a part of this. John kept waiting, soon the sounds of pots and pans from the kitchen told him she was making dinner. In between she came out into the living room, right in front of the closet John was hiding in, and began folding laundry. She paced back and forth from chore to chore, visible through tiny ventilation slits in the closet door. John looked down at his daughter hiding next to him, even though she was dead. He knew she was dead, but she was also right there with him. He tried not to think of it, thinking of what he did to her. Sometimes when he looked at her she would ask why daddy was so sad. He made her drink the cup, that's why he was sad.

Ellen walked towards the closet with a furry crimson jacket in her hand, the one that had been draped across a chair. John had been wondering when she would open the closet to put it away, forcing him to act before he was ready. John didn't want to be found yet. Ellen reached for the closet door and then stopped as sounds of overflowing boiling water swelled from the kitchen. The jacket lay on the floor now. She hurried to the kitchen and disappeared from view.

John opened the closet door and stepped into the soft glow of an iridescent lamp, exposing him inside Ellen's house. He was too large to move quickly. He grabbed the sport jacket and slipped back inside the closet, carefully shutting the door before Ellen returned. She didn't need to know yet.

John's neural mapping allowed him to read minds, clear as a painting. The moment a person was within arm's reach of him, he felt their emotions and could read their thoughts. He could see everything in their conscious mind, it was a function of his programming, one he couldn't control. When John tortured Kayd's son, Jack Lad, he had felt everything. He felt the pain, felt the fear, the despair, felt it like it was happening to him. He felt the moment Kayd accepted the reality of killing his son. John knew that feeling personally. Part of him was aware that it didn't make sense, he shouldn't be able to do those things. He shouldn't even be alive.

"Daddy," she sighed impatiently.

"Phonm should be home soon, please sweetheart, stay quiet for me," John whispered.

Phonm Ngu was harder to find than the others. He had been an Elite Officer under Jack Sethren, and he had led part of the genocide on Space Station Hephaestus. John knew, because that's where it all happened, that's where John killed his own family, and John remembered seeing Phonm's face. John caught a glimpse of Phonm and four other Elites that day. As it turned out, they all came to New Seattle City to lead peaceful lives, working for Sethren Company, rinsing blood off their hands ever since.

Tracking Phonm was like tracking a rabbit two days into a blizzard. Most of his records were so altered or erased that John had to cross reference the most basic of addresses and numbers just to find they didn't exist or someone else actually lived there instead. As head of security he had many ways to make himself disappear. But even Phonm wasn't untraceable, if you had the time. John had lots of time. Funny, how he survived all this time. How did I survive? I must have died…

Error...runreset.exe//...   ...

John had blacked out for one hour, forty three minutes, and three seconds. He awoke in the middle of doing something. He hated waking up this way, running or chasing, his body operating on its own. But this wasn't the first time that had happened. When John awoke he was towering over Phonm. Phonm was wearing black silk pajamas, paralyzed with fear, holding a sandwich as if it were a shield. John wasn't sure when Phonm had come home, but he knew to the millisecond how long he was blacked out.

Phonm suddenly found his feet and ran for what it was worth, trying to escape. John caught him in two strides, chunks of plaster raining down where his head scraped the ceiling. Phonm screamed out wordlessly, dangling in John's grip. Phonm's thoughts were ragged and didn't make any sense. Phonm thought he saw a robot, or an android. John didn't understand that. Fear must be warping Phonm's thoughts.

He could have killed him right there, he wanted to rip him apart. It took great willpower not to. Killing Phonm wasn't enough. Death was not the ultimate punishment. John's agonizing existence in the cargo lock taught him that. For some things, death was a mercy. For Phonm, Kayd, and the others, John would show them how terrible *living* could be. How terrible making the right choice could be. How terrible it was to kill someone you loved. John had used the thirty years in a frozen cargo hold to design his revenge. How did I survive the cold? No food? Error//runexec.bat...

...reboot...
Not again...

John woke up again. Ellen Ngu, Phonm's wife, was tied up. John blacked out for twelve minutes and thirteen seconds. He had blacked out, but he knew he was the one who tied her up even if he couldn't remember doing it. Ellen was in a chair with her hands brutally nailed into the armrests. Phonm was in another chair, forced to watch. Forced to choose how she would die. Phonm would learn today if he could do what John *had* to do.

"Please...you don't have to do this..." Phonm begged.
"Spare her from the pain."

"...please," Ellen whimpered, "please... Phonm... just do it..." she begged him. The pool of blood widened at the base of the chair. Phonm pounded his fists against the table.

"I can't. I can't!!" he cried. "Please, tell me why!!" he screamed at John.

John wouldn't answer. Phonm looked down, finally accepting the truth of his situation. John sensed the changes occur, his brain patterns, recognition, Phonm knew he was being punished. His forgotten past had found him, and he knew. So much fear and emotion came through Phonm that John had to step back, his sensors were overloading. John sensed Phonm was mustering the resolve to do it, to kill his wife Ellen, who John knew he loved very much. Phonm looked at his hands, and then at Ellen. She was in so much pain, begging to die for the relief it would bring. This was John's revenge, the moment between indecision and action, where the terrible choice was embraced. Death wasn't enough, they had to know the pain he knew. They had to deliberately hurt the ones they loved, to protect them from something far worse.

And Phonm really loved her. By the pain on Phonm's face, in his eyes, and by the way his body shook it was evident that he loved her, John knew this even without his sensors. Phonm stood and picked up the knife. He walked over to his wife under John's careful gaze. Ellen had the strength to look away, beneath her pain John sensed relief that it would soon be over. Phonm held the knife, testing the handle in his grip. He held the blade in front of her, he readied his hand to do it, one clean thrust to the heart, instant and final. But when his shoulders slumped down, Ellen's emotions changed and she began to cry. "I just can't..." he finally said. Phonm looked at her, in his eyes he apologized to her. *The coward...* Ellen wept in fear of the pain she was about to suffer. In this John knew that the choice he made long ago, the terrible pain of giving his wife and children lethal doses of potassium laced juice, was the correct choice. Phonm wasn't as strong as John was, and he had chosen poorly because of it.

Taylor had consciously blocked out everything from his childhood. There was nothing he kept as a token, no

memory or recollection he ever reminisced. He survived his childhood, and for good reason never thought of it again. But subconsciously he had no control. No escape from the replays that happened deep into his sleep cycles. He suffered them frequently, though rarely did the memories linger once his eyes were open. Right now, his eyes were not open, and he was an eight year old boy again, in elementary school, waiting for something terrible to happen. He heard a voice.

"Taylor, turn away from the wall now," Mrs. Critchett said. Taylor stepped away from the wall and glared across the classroom at the other children. "Taylor, don't glare or I'll swat you again," she warned.

"Can I go to my seat?" he asked, stuffing tiny hands into his pants pockets.

"What's the magic word?"

Taylor squirmed. "Please"

"Please what?!" she snapped, hands on her hips. Her bottom lip stretched taught.

Taylor kept his hands from trembling. "May I please go to my seat?"

"Of course you can, child," sweet as honey.

Taylor walked across the classroom to his seat, all eyes were on him. He had a hard time walking when everyone watched him. He also had to pee real bad, but he knew the teacher would say no if he asked. He always tried to be good, but it seemed like the more he tried the worse trouble he got in. But today was actually a really good day. He got to sit next to Jenny.

Usually she sat in the back of class and the teacher always made him sit in the front, but today he sat next to her. Nothing could make this a bad day since he got to sit next to Jenny. Yesterday he smiled at her and she didn't smile back. Taylor had felt like a fool all night because of it. He barely touched his dinner at the orphanage because he was so embarrassed. But then today Jenny wanted to sit by him. For once he did something right. He really did want to be good.

As he walked up to his seat he smiled a toothy grin and gave Jenny a little wave. She was smiling back at him, but she didn't wave. That's okay, she still smiled. She was so pretty, Taylor wanted to marry her. He walked up to his seat and as he sat down something horrible bit him.

"OW!" he cried, leaping off the seat. A small needle jutted out of the seat, taped in place. He rubbed his bottom in pain. He felt blood. He didn't like blood, it always made him feel icky. Everyone in the classroom started laughing, Taylor couldn't hold his pee anymore and it pooled on the floor next to his feet. They laughed even louder. "Hey, I guess orphans aren't potty trained!" fat Tommy shouted. "He peed himself!" someone else yelled. Everyone laughed so loud.

"His own momma didn't want him," a girl snickered. Taylor looked at the teacher to do something. She should stop this, she should protect him, but instead she shielded a laugh with her hand. Taylor shook. Jenny was laughing too, giggling with the girl next to her. He ran out of the classroom and into the hallway, feet echoed as he sped from the hallway to the door outside. He could barely breathe as he ran out into the cold winter air, tears blocking his vision. The worst part, his shoes squeaked from being wet with pee. With each running step it squeaked louder, shouting his shame, laughing at him even more. He was sprinting now, down the street, against the cold air and grey sky, and he had nowhere to run. He made it to the Market Stop before falling against the building in tears. Today was going so well! He had been happy all morning! He thought Jenny liked him, but she didn't, she just wanted to play a trick on him. He hated himself. He hated being laughed at. He hated his stupid shoes for squeaking, so he took them off and threw them into an abandoned lot next to the Market Stop. He almost threw his pants there too. He stared at the huge,

wide, wet spot where he peed himself. What was he going to do about these pants? He couldn't take them off and walk around naked, that would make everyone laugh at him even more. Taylor grabbed his pants in frustration, he pulled so hard his fingers hurt. He always tried to do the right thing, and it never worked for him. He didn't understand why everything went wrong for him. He just wanted to be a good kid.

||Chapter 6||

"Ow... ... ... Shit..."

The real world came knocking, ending Taylor's coma. He had been dreaming. Taylor had dreams like that sometimes, just another of life's little courtesies. With an unyieldingly stiff neck he twisted to check the time on his wrist, forcing half an eye open with all his might. 10:15 in the morning. He looked at his phone that had been buried into his rib a few moments ago. He had four messages and eleven missed calls, he was popular today.

Taylor stood as normally as he could, or meant to when he stepped on something and cried out in pain. Rubbing his eyes he looked down to see his bare feet, he had stepped on a shard of hard plastic. He was wearing shoes last night. He wiggled his toes, as if asking them if they really didn't have shoes on them. They were bare, and Taylor didn't know when this occurred. He thought for a moment, trying to recollect, wondering where his shoes were. He looked around, hoping he kicked them off when he curled up to sleep…in the alleyway. But he didn't see them anywhere. Taylor sighed. At least it didn't rain last night. He gingerly set his foot down, all the while moaning like a woman in labor and hung over. The soreness of sleeping on pavement reached its way into his upper back, he wouldn't be comfortable for hours as he twisted and stretched. And then it popped into his head, the report Keeb wanted this morning, the report he had not thought about until right now. Damn. Double damn. "I need a cigarette," he said, wishfully feeling his pockets.

Still trying to accept the fact that he was alive and standing he brushed the wrinkles off his pants and reached into his pockets. Nothing was missing aside from his shoes. His shirt clung to his body and he suffered from a fierce thirst. His kidneys were intact. That was good. But he would have preferred his shoes, those were custom.

Taylor stumbled out of the alleyway to the harsh pavement of the city. The soles of his feet seared against the sun-baked sidewalk with each step. His feet were too delicate for this, he was going to have raw skin for a week. Though no one was looking at him he endured imaginary eyes. A group of kids on a field trip shared the sidewalk with him, until the teacher steered them clear of Taylor. Taylor shut his eyes for a moment. This was way too much commotion for him right now. Too many people moving, too much happening. He took a breath and opened his eyes again.

"Geez," he admitted, looking at his reflection in a shop window. He looked rough. For a moment he didn't even recognize himself, his hair was spiked to the side and his clothes were wrinkled beyond recognition. Small chance anyone would recognize him, not even a cop. He quickly searched for his badge, letting out a moan of relief upon finding it. He would have had a hard time explaining how he lost it already.

Each step scorched and sent a renewed ache through his body as he worked his way to a nearby transit station. He seemingly stepped on pebbles, cracks, little pieces of glass, and nameless goo. "I can't believe I lost my shoes," he moaned. His back cramped, forcing him to walk like an undead drunk. The police station was only five blocks away, which was still too far. The transit would have to do, the thought of walking five blocks was on the same level as the thought of walking five hundred miles. He needed to get there and fill out the report Keeb wanted over an hour ago.

He picked his spot in line behind a well-to-do heavyset man. His suit was a fine navy blue but he smelled like a broken bottle of cologne hid in his pocket. Taylor stood right behind him, so close he could see the quality fibers of the man's coat. This was taking way too long. He had to get to work and fill out that damn report before Keeb noticed it wasn't there yet. Assuming he would be so lucky.

"Ahem," the stranger coughed and stepped out of line. Taylor looked at him for a moment, wondering. He then lifted his arm up and discretely smelled himself. *What*? He may have smelled a little bit. At least the transit arrived before anyone else fell out of line. He boarded and plopped to a white plastic seat when the doors finally opened. The seat cushion was shredded and penned across, and felt wet in a way that should have bothered him. He lost the strength to hold his head upright, leaning it against the plexiwindow. He looked up at some graffiti on the ceiling.

LAUGHTER LOVE HAPPINESS

"Whatever," Taylor mumbled. What was he even going to say in this stupid report? Maybe he could just copy one and turn it in. Thinking hurt way too much right now.

A beggar woman in a hodgepodge of rags shared the cabin with them, she got up and approached a younger couple three seats forward, asking them for money. The boyfriend looked uncomfortable, yet he sensed an opportunity to show his girlfriend how compassionate he was, in an obvious effort to impress her. Taylor judged they were a new couple, maybe a week long, yet he wasn't sure how he came up with that. The boyfriend reached into his pocket and handed the beggar a bit of cash. The beggar then started coming towards Taylor. Taylor quickly feigned sleep, abhorring the thought of her talking to him. There was a chance she would just pass by.

Tap tap

Taylor glared. What the hell was wrong with people, didn't she see him pretending to sleep? The woman carried a soft yet needy grin and smelled worse than he did. She held a picture of a baby with some phony message scribbled underneath it. She did not speak, seemingly could not. Taylor waved her off, but she still stood in front of him.

"What?!" he demanded.

"Please..."

"Leave me alone," Taylor said. He wouldn't read the

message on the picture. It probably wasn't true, any of it, he doubted she even had a baby. The beggar finally left, and when she did Taylor caught a glance of an elderly woman scowling at him.

"What's with you old people??" Taylor yelled, wishing he hadn't. Taylor decided to shut his eyes the rest of the way, to hell with everything else. Why did Keeb have to ask for this stupid report? Detectives had a reputation for being on their own time, thanks to the urban legend 'Duke' among others. Keeb must not have gotten that history lesson. Before he could daydream more than that, the transit came to a halt at Taylor's stop. He left the transit, ignoring everything except the art of walking in pain, and he carefully made his way up the hard, wide steps to Precinct Four. Once Taylor was inside he finally felt a little relief. He raised his chin, propped his shoulders back, and walked barefoot through the lobby.

The receptionist, Jane, looked ready to call for security before she recognized him. Taylor approached the armored door, digging in his pockets for the clearance key. "Jane, have you done something to your hair?" he asked. She looked terrified that he had spoken to her, and to get him out of view she pressed the access button. After that, she flipped through files on her desk, refusing to look up.

Bitch. Only new employees ever greeted Taylor. He didn't know why. He limped down the hallway to his office, he could fill out this report in two minutes, as long as handwriting wasn't an issue. Officer Grolsch's friend, whose name he never remembered, seemingly couldn't make enough room as they passed each other in the hallway. His office door was just steps away, already he smelled Catheri's perfume. After the report he would be one shower away from becoming a new man.

Taylor looked at Catheri, too tired to give the usual wink, but still able to notice her low cut top.

"Good morning, Detective," she said, unusually professional. Something was up. With his office door open, Taylor saw Vina inside, plainly dressed in a peach skirt, waiting for him. Vina looked angry in a way Taylor had never seen.

"Where have you been?" she demanded, containing an emotion that was so clearly on her face.

Taylor didn't have time for this. He needed to fill out that damn report before Keeb checked on it. What was she doing here? "I told you, I was working a case. An all-nighter," Taylor's migraine threatened to come back. He had to get rid of her, and fast.

"You look like hell," Vina said. "I was worried! You should have called---"

Taylor snatched her arm, pulling her close and lowering his voice to a threat. He squeezed her until it hurt, though that part was unintentional. "Don't *ever* come here. Go home, clean the house, you will see me when you see me," he said through clenched teeth.

Vina stared at Taylor for a moment, her face trying to comprehend what she just witnessed. She was in shock that he would treat her like that. In a way, it was the first time they had made eye contact, the first time she had seen the real him at least. It was a little too uncomfortable for Taylor, he suddenly wanted to apologize, something he never did. Her eyes filled with tears. Her mouth opened but no words came out. Taylor turned and organized files on his desk. From the corner of his eye he saw her try to stand tall and leave, only to trip in front of Catheri's desk. Her purse spilled out across the floor. Catheri quickly helped Vina pick up her scattered belongings, it was odd to see them working together, his wife and his mistress. Catheri was jealous of Vina, Vina didn't know anything about Catheri, and there they were, side by side. A fleeting thought of a three-way came and went. He had no control over that part of his brain. Vina never should have come here. He turned to ignore them both.

Taylor shut the door when his phone rang, he answered it before thinking. "Detective Taylor speaking." He could not have sounded shorter.

"Detective. Did you forget about me?" Keeb said over the phone.

Taylor slapped his forehead. Apparently, Keeb noticed the report wasn't there yet. "I've been working all night, boss," he said rubbing the skin off his face trying to wake up. Again he needed to be careful when lying to Keeb.

"Did my assignment get in the way of your fun?"
"No sir," Taylor said.

"So you completed the report?"

"Of course, sir," Taylor said, wishing he hadn't.

"Then I really don't know why your report isn't here."

"I'll have to talk to my assistant, sir, she was supposed to turn it in. I'll just do another report, sorry about the mixup," Taylor said.

Keeb was silent for a moment. It was bullshit and they both knew it, Taylor waited to be called out on it.

"Perhaps. Now, it's a new day, and there is a new murder."

"What? Where?" Taylor gladly directed the focus off himself, though he was also a little surprised. Keeb wasn't the kind of Commander who accepted mistakes.

"Catheri just received an attachment, you have five minutes to get here. This was your freebie, Detective. You don't get another."

Keeb was one commander in New Seattle City whose threats were not ignored. Taylor wouldn't be surprised if he had a jar full of testicles somewhere from cops who disappointed him. The call ended and Taylor's lower left desk drawer slid open. He grabbed a shot of *nitrous9* and scribbled Kayd Lad's name on a piece of paper, handed it to Catheri, and told her to file it. As Taylor bolted, he knew Catheri would look at the report and fill in the rest for him. She was that kind of girl. He streamed past Vina in the hallway, trying to organize her purse, or her life. They looked one in the same right now.

It took Taylor four and a half minutes, he had ordered special transport by a Patrol Unit. Upper Bellevue was a neighborhood designed to make the common man feel inadequate. The smoggy grit of downtown, so prevalent that it's part of the décor, faded away here to an endless stretch of million dollar lawns. The patrol car from the YARD came to a stop. The rider had turned off his swirling lights several blocks ago to keep the important Citizens here feeling safe.

43 Romero Drive. Taylor breathed in and exhaled slowly. Another murder. The homeowner, a Mr. Phonm Ngu, was supposedly still inside the house. Taylor stepped out of the car and onto the sidewalk, the patrol car zipped away without so much as a wave. Taylor smirked, the rider had tried every excuse not to drive Taylor. Everyone in Precinct Four hated him, it seemed. Taylor managed to convince him though, he just mentioned something about Keeb being disappointed.

Crime-scene lasers erected a solid green perimeter at the walkway to 43 Romero, blipping as Taylor walked through. Detective badges gave clearance by way of an embedded computer chip. Taylor wasn't ready for what he saw, and he wasn't even inside yet. From the doorstep to the ceiling, a spiral blood trail guided him inside the open door. He followed as the blood grew from little red dots to brush strokes. Taylor kept his distance for fear of staining his clothes.

Commander Keeb was inside. Again? He stood over someone, a man in a chair with his arms meekly folded.

An officer filled out forms in the other room, a spacious and well decorated room that Taylor might have noticed if he wasn't terrified of getting blood on his clothes. How many people died here? And what was Keeb still doing out of his office? Taylor noticed an uneaten sandwich on the floor. On the far side of the room an investigator was documenting blood splatter, a job that would take him all night.

The man sitting at the table may as well have been unaware of the Officers in the room, he spoke to himself in gibberish, almost in a trance-like state. He must be the owner, Phonm, but since no one else was paying him any attention Taylor wasn't about to start. Taylor looked around the dining area at an antique sword on the wall, then at some decorative cups on a shelf. There was a wallet and several key cards on the table, and a small porcelain cat on the windowsill. Then he saw a picture frame cycling digital photos, and one caught Taylor's attention. The photo showed Phonm, in a happier time obviously, standing side by side with Jack Sethren, the one and only. Taylor paused. Phonm was acquaintances with the most powerful man in New Seattle City?

"He says a *cyborg* tried to make him kill his wife, but he couldn't do it, so the *cyborg* killed her instead," Keeb said, looking down at Taylor over the rim of his glasses.

"This is from one body?" Taylor said looking at the blood. His stomach leaned to the side, threatening to turn over on him. He shook it off. "A killer cyborg, that's a good one," Taylor quietly mocked. He would be so lucky, except cyborgs didn't exist anymore. Very little of what was called 'high tech' survived the Second Darkening. And while Sethren Company was leading the way in bringing those technologies back, they certainly never showcased anything that exotic. Then Taylor realized the important part of what Keeb said, that the assailant tried to get Phonm to kill his own wife. Just like Kayd Lad, being forced to kill his own son. Keeb waited to see that recognition dawn on Taylor, and when it did he continued.

"There may be a connection, obviously, but I'm not about to put out an alert for a cyborg. Not when I have this. Here," Keeb held out a file. Taylor grabbed it and flipped through its glossy pages.

"A suspect?" Taylor tried not to laugh. "Already?" Taylor might as well have asked the wall. Keeb probably had a suspect before this morning's coffee. In a way Taylor wasn't surprised, the department had a reputation of public safety to uphold. They would always find somebody to arrest for a murder, whether or not the person actually did it. Keeb continued.

"This house belongs to Phonm Ngu, retired head of security from Sethren Company, instrumental in designing the security systems for Sethren Tower. He is delusional, obviously, a cyborg didn't kill his wife."

"Sir, he and Kayd were both high ranking employees at Sethren Company. We should put out some kind of an alert," Taylor suggested.

"Don't be ridiculous," Keeb said.

"Ridiculous?" Taylor asked. What was ridiculous about warning potential murder victims?

"That would cause unnecessary problems for the staff at Sethren Company," Keeb said turning halfway to the door. "I have to go now, but I'm expecting you to make the arrest this afternoon." He glared while speaking, giving his command a wordless threat. Taylor got it loud and clear.

Sure boss, Taylor thought. He whistled through his teeth. What the hell was this? He knew he was being used, which Taylor didn't really have a problem with, that was almost part of the deal, but he needed to know what he was being used for. Something was being covered up, something involving people who didn't want their reputations publicly smeared. But what? What would make Keeb himself come down and handle things directly?

Phonm continued to mumble, to himself or to the

Officer next to him, Taylor wasn't sure. Taylor walked through the house. The rooms were a stark contrast to the crowded spaces and worn, artificial furnishings his line of work usually took him too. The hallway flowed from the entertaining area, he noticed bits of plaster sat on the wood flooring. The ceiling had been badly scraped, twice, and it happened recently judging by the mess. The closet to Taylor's right looked like an ape burst loose from inside of it, the hinges were bent and the doors didn't close properly. Taylor judged that had happened recently as well. Returning from the entertainment room Taylor happened to glance upon something, something he was sure was supposed to be missed. A throw rug had been scooted aside during last night's events, the fine lines of a trap door were just barely visible.

"Hey guys," Taylor said, motioning an Officer to him.

"Yes, Detective?" came the apprehensive reply.

But something told Taylor to keep quiet. He already had his orders, a suspect, the one Keeb had given him, and he didn't want anyone to report back that he was actually still investigating. For now, Taylor was content to appear as the puppet, just like the one Keeb was expecting him to be. Taylor paused, hovering between what to do. "Ah, watch out for all the blood. Don't disturb the scene," Taylor said.

The Officer stared at him. "Good tip," he said and quickly got back to ignoring Taylor. Taylor checked the light switches. Somewhere there would be a button or a hidden key box. When he finally checked behind a painting of Phonm's wife he found a nondescript key panel. Gently laying the painting to the floor he examined the hidden panel, Precinct Four used similar ones. Taylor asked himself what he was doing, did he really want to know anything more than what Keeb wanted him to know? Besides, this was looking suspiciously like real work.

Lucky for him, detectives were issued key breakers. All electronic security systems were, by law, required to accept government key breakers as override codes. This was the first time Taylor got to use one on *official* business. Unofficially he had used them many times. He ducked his head around to make sure no one was watching.

He inserted the key breaker, and nothing happened.

Phonm disabled government access, Taylor mused. Phonm would certainly know how. He recalled that Sethren Company held security contracts with the government, police obviously included. This sort of equipment was worth two years in prison. Taylor gently rubbed the side of his face. A feeling simmered in the pit of Taylor's stomach, one that bespoke of danger, of buried secrets that should be ignored, of answers only a fool would seek. Taylor called his office from his telecom piece.

"Detective Taylor's office," Catheri said from the other line.

"Catheri, I need you to do something for me." Taylor spoke in hushed tones as he continued his inspection of Phonm's house, placing the painting back on the wall. He wasn't really sure of what he was doing.

]]Chapter 7[[

Catheri was still frustrated that her son Jaek had hung up on her, she didn't even finish what she was saying. She had called to cancel dinner because of Taylor's unusual request. Catheri groaned in frustration. Her son Jaek just didn't understand. Catheri widened her step down the hallway to the elevator.

"Morning Charlie," she chimed as she walked by the admin room, donning a smile. The elevator took her down to the sub basement Supply Room. Locked doors littered the hallway and ended with a reinforced half glass door. She never understood why there was more security here than anywhere else in the precinct. A blob, Specialist Connor, emerged from behind the counter. The unfortunate soul didn't see daylight often; for the best of her she never remembered a time that he wasn't there. He worked weekends, never took a sick day, not one vacation. His stomach protruded over his belt buckle as he sat, sweat glistened off his brow.

"Hello Connor," Catheri smiled. *The years have not been kind*, she thought. She recalled a drunken indiscretion with him over four years ago. She shuddered at the thought of it now, his body on top of hers, though at the time it *was* a different body. At least since that night she never had a problem getting gear from him.

"Catheri! Hey, you don't visit enough!" He used to be handsome, until he discovered artificial meats.

"Connor, there just aren't enough opportunities. I'm here for the Spec7."

He met her with a long sideways look. "For what?"
"Official business of course," she smiled.
"Sure, why not... first let me wipe the dust off," he sighed and slid from the seat, a great relief to the quarter

inch foam padding underneath. She shuddered again. He returned moments later, dusting off what looked like an ordinary briefcase. The Spec7 was a clandestine cyber device capable of simultaneously hacking and copying electronic data within twenty meters; computers, digital key panels, etc. Too sophisticated for its own good, it hadn't been used in a decade.

"Hey, you going to the yacht party Saturday?" Connor never gave up trying for another night with her. Sadly such persistence had paid off for him. *Once*. Catheri just smiled.

"Plans," she winked and headed out before Connor could invite her somewhere else.

With the Spec7 in tow she ascended the elevators, hustled down the hallway, and left the precinct. The low sun hit her eyes without conviction, the day was ending. And as she had done far too often, she went to the transit station underground and readied to board the lightrail. Always the lightrail. She spent so much time either waiting for one, or riding on one. With all the requirements to license a private vehicle hardly anyone bothered to drive anymore. But as Sethren Company reminded you, who needed POV's when you could ride the lightrails? Without access to personal vehicles the lightrail was part of daily life, eventually she would get used to it. Eventually. Sethren Company championed it as the most efficient mass transportation system ever designed, for all Catheri knew, maybe it was.

Catheri made her way to 43 Romero Dr. just as Taylor instructed her to, though he would be gone by now. He had called hours ago and told her to wait until evening. She felt like she didn't belong in such a nice place, as if she wasn't good enough to walk these sidewalks. But maybe one day, she told herself. Of course she dreamed of living somewhere like this, her and Taylor and Jaek could be happy here.

She found the address. No cars, no police, no lights on inside. She felt like a burglar. The front door was unlocked, just as Taylor said it would be. The lights were off but Catheri could see blood all over the walls. She tried to ignore that and found the corner of the entertaining room. She set the briefcase down, activating it with the push of a button. It was supposed to take a minute, and in that time the Spec7 would disable all locks, hack and copy files on nearby computers, and do it without being detected. It would take sixty seconds, she started counting in her head. At seven seconds the key panel hidden behind the painting activated.

"Just like he said," she shrugged. The doorway in the floor opened when she pushed the button on the key panel. A hole in the floor appeared ominously, Catheri found herself peering down in it as underground lights activated, revealing a ladder and a metallic room. From above she could see an antiquated collection of weapons lining the wall. She would have to climb down for a better look. She hated being the tool of Taylor's curiosity. She went down the ladder.

There were rifles and insignia from both sides of the war hanging on the walls, proudly alongside officer arms, blasters, plasma grenades, graphite bayonets, insignia of various units from skirmishes over the last hundred years. Impressive as it was, it didn't require an illegal security system and a special underground room. "Oh," she said, her hand covering her mouth. Then she saw it. On the far end of the wall was a uniform on display like a shrine, a uniform that struck fear even now as it surely did then; the upside down trident on the collar, a chapter of history in need of being erased. It captured her so much it took Catheri a moment to realize there were dozens of human skulls on the floor beneath it.

"God…" she uttered. This was the uniform of an Elite officer, an infamous death unit from the old UMA. She actually wanted to run, but she couldn't look away from it.

The presence of that uniform was enough to make her a coward. Her paralysis was interrupted by voices coming from above.

"Yeah yeah, I forget shit all the time. Don't worry, my wife reminds me," the man's voice carried well. He talked like a cop, Catheri knew because she heard it all day long. She pulled herself up the ladder and slapped the key panel to make the trap door close with an agonizing lack of urgency. The front door to the house swung open.

"Damn Eddy, you forget to lock the door too??" a different voice asked.

"Fuck no," he said. The two cops fell silent.

Catheri's heart beat louder than she could think. She snatched the Spec7 and nearly fell over with it as she dodged a center coffee table. She scooted into the kitchen, looking for somewhere to hide. She couldn't let herself get caught, Taylor would never forgive her.

A light near the door switched on. Catheri heard footsteps coming slowly towards the kitchen. Carefully she tiptoed, wishing the Spec7 weighed less, backtracking into the living room. She couldn't just run for the door, they would catch her before she hit the street outside. She was having a hard time hearing which way they went. If they came down the hallway she could try to leave through the kitchen. If they came through the kitchen, she'd backtrack through the hallway. Somehow all of this made the main door feel impossibly far away. How much trouble was she in if they did find her? She heard something, a small foot scuff, coming towards the kitchen. She quietly slipped closer to the hallway, praying the two Officers didn't split up.

"Is anybody in here?"

The Spec7 was getting heavier by the second, so she set her free hand on the counter and felt something slick. Whoever made dinner last had left an oily basil mess on the counter without cleaning it up. Catheri heard the safety button on a service blaster click loose. The echoing sound made her regret ever answering Taylor's phone call tonight. Catheri leaned her head slowly around the corner of the hallway, there were two shadows and she saw the door was left slightly open. She went halfway down the hall, keeping her eye on the two shadows of the Officers heading into the kitchen. Their shadows stopped moving. If they headed back, she would be caught. Could she slip out from under their noses? She wished they would go deeper into the kitchen. Another light came on and Catheri jumped, too terrified to move.

"Come on, there's no one," she heard the baritone voiced Officer say. Catheri watched as the two Officers visibly relaxed, though all she could see were their shadows. They headed through the kitchen, which gave her an opening for the door, but also a deadline. If she didn't move now, they would find her standing in the hallway. Catheri wanted to sprint, but instead she tiptoed, silently, praying she could leave without being found. She didn't know what she would say if they found her.

She never felt freer as she slipped past the door. She exited the house finally, walking down the stone pathway to the street, still expecting to be caught even though she was finally outside. All they had to do was look out the window and they would see her. She tried to suppress her walk, it was everything she could do to keep from running. Her adrenaline pumped. When she hit the sidewalk she thought she heard their voices again. She couldn't take it anymore and ran, bouncing the Spec7 like a briefcase full of bricks. She ran from more than just those two Officers. The upside-down trident of the Elites was burning in her mind.

]]Chapter 8[[

The sun imposed the last of its will on New Seattle City. Giants grew from the shadows of tall buildings, and those who walked towards the setting sun were blinded by it. Every damn night. Taylor had tried four types of window shades before finding ones that kept his office dark. He was waiting for Catheri, so far he had paced the room seven times with the lights off and tripped twice.

He cursed himself for sending Catheri there. He did not often admit mistakes, but she could not be replaced if something went wrong, and worse, he was stuck here waiting for her to return. He looked again outside, parting the blinds ever so slightly, squinting at the orange ball stalled on the horizon. He could barely tell what he was looking at, but he would know if he saw Catheri. He'd see heads turning as she walked by.

A squat man on the sidewalk had been outside for too long, seemingly doing nothing. The man made Taylor uneasy. Taylor again looked outside. The man was gone. What was he thinking? Paranoia was getting the better of him.

Taylor closed his eyes, set his hands out flat on the window sill. What was he worrying about? He shook his head. Sethren Company or not, he'd be fine. It's not like they had men on every street corner waiting for someone like Taylor to poke their nose around. He shrugged. "The dye is ca--" the word froze as Taylor's blaster spun out of the holster, aimed on the door ready to fire. Something made him do that. His imagination, maybe, but he held still nonetheless. Then, ever so slightly, the door handle turned, so subtle he shouldn't have noticed it.

Catheri would knock. His chest beat harder. The door creaked open and let in a beam of artificial light. "Taylor?"

"Catheri!" Taylor whispered. "What took you so

long?" he snapped, both angry and relieved.

"Why are you in the dark?" Catheri whispered back.

"Were you followed?" he whispered again.

"Why are we whispering?" she asked. Taylor shrugged. With a thud she slumped against the doorway, happy to finally relax. The Spec7 clanked to the ground like a large brick.

"Well?" he asked.

"You could say thanks! I peed myself in there," Catheri huffed and flipped on the lights. Taylor rubbed his eyes before looking at her.

"Thanks, good job. What did you find?"

"Nothing... just a bunch of childhood junk," she said. She turned to the coat rack dismissing further conversation as she untied her jacket.

"What??" Taylor had a hard time believing Phonm went to so much trouble for some family keepsakes.

"One man's garbage is another man's treasure. So they say," she slouched against the wall even further.

Taylor crossed the room and grabbed the briefcase from her. Catheri let her gaze fall. "What are you doing?" she asked nervously.

"What do you think I'm doing?" he asked back. Catheri fought against her nerves. She didn't know what was on Phonm's computer, but hopefully there was nothing about what she saw down there. Taylor didn't need to know what was down there, no one needed to know. That part of history needed to disappear.

"Taylor, about tonight... you can come over--" Catheri began.

"Can't, I'm busy," he cut her short.

Taylor looked at her again. "Well, what I mean is, Keeb wants a full report by morning," he smiled and set the briefcase down. In two steps he pulled her in close, wrapping his arms around her, driving his hands down across the small of her back.

"Did Keeb really ask you to do this? I mean with the Spec7?"

"Of course," he said, letting her go abruptly. In the rarest moments where Taylor did try to show affection, he expected it in return. "Hit the lights as you go."

Catheri knew she had just been dismissed, she hated how Taylor's moods could shift so quickly. "I wish this cyber crap never came back," she paused, watching the Spec7 load onboard software. She prayed nothing about the Elites was in any of Phonm's files. The door closed as silently as her leaving.

Loading...

Taylor waited as the monitor warmed up. Monochrome green data-bits streamed into dozens, hundreds, and then thousands of files. He wiped away dust as he waited, corners of the screen had deadened from years of sitting. It asked for a password, Taylor used the department password: *NSC1247*. When it finished compiling the data Taylor's hopes sagged. Thousands of unorganized files displayed onscreen. Appointments, research, planning, shipping documents, invoices, receipts, expense accounts, the list went on. This was more than just Phonm's personal computer data.

Sethren Company files, Taylor realized. That was where Phonm worked, after all. Taylor thumbed his nose. It was bad juju to pry on Sethren Company. A wise man would delete everything, put away the Spec7, change his name and appearance, and never think on it again.

Aimlessly he opened one; RWSAP.bak, a record about shipped copper from a cable warehouse to the Tech Department. Taylor tapped his desk with a pen. He was in far deeper than he intended to get. Stealing files from Sethren Company was unintentional, he was just looking for whatever Phonm was hiding. He wouldn't have sent Catheri if he could have done it himself, but Keeb had his eye all over him. Taylor sensed that Kayd and Phonm's cases may be connected, Sethren Company being the obvious clue, but more importantly he sensed it may go deeper than he was willing to go. Well, if both murders were linked to Sethren Company, it was probably best to follow Keeb's lead. As soon as Taylor knew what Phonm was hiding that would be the end of his curiosity.

"Wow. Copper." He spotted a search menu in the lower corner of the screen, an inkling worked its way into his brain.

"What the hell was that guy's name," Taylor thought a moment before typing it in.

[[Kayd Lad: result ... No file.]]

"No file on a senior employee?" Taylor mused. He tried again.

[[Phonm Ngu: result ... No file.]]

Taylor leaned back, bringing his left hand to his lip in thought. The Spec7 stole information about mundane copper materials but not their senior employees? This was beginning to look like it didn't belong to Sethren Company after all. Maybe Phonm was a corporate spy, and he got caught? Taylor tried again.

[[Show> Employee List: result ...]]

Three hundred and forty seven names appeared, starting with Olgi Aalder, a janitor of six months on floor three in the Sethren Maintenance Dept, age 37, diagnosed hypoglycemic. That answers that question... "I need to rethink this," Taylor announced to no one in particular.

Taylor thought best when moving, so he walked to the drinking fountain down the hallway, irritated by something nameless, trying to clear his head. He paced the hallway and let his mind wander. Everything about these two murders fit like square blocks in a round puzzle. Taylor found himself staring at a janitor's closet.

"Oh hell, why bother?" he asked, collapsing in small defeat. This wasn't necessary. He wasn't really going to investigate these murders anyway, not if he didn't have to. He knew the best thing for his career, and his sanity, was to arrest Keeb's puppet suspect and wait for further instruction. That was the plan! Taylor looked back at his office. He just had to know what Phonm was hiding first...

Taylor never had a knack for focus. Resisting the urge to sit down he wandered, cursing the uselessness of the Spec7. No one ever used the damn thing, it was from a time before the Darkening. Most of the stuff the Spec7 did didn't even make sense, too much technobabble that must have been common place once. Of course, some things came back. Long lost gizmos, research papers that were too advanced to make sense, nano-tools that somehow endured the wars. Usually no one knew how to use it or what it did. And other times, like A-Grav technology, it made life better and made someone else richer.

That brought his train of thought to Sethren Company, which seemingly built their empire on lost technologies. He had finished pacing the hallway and plopped back into his seat in his office. He just wanted to know what Phonm was hiding, then it was off to bed. He felt like he had to remind himself of that, he had to remind himself that he could care less who the real killer was. The real Taylor didn't care, never did. This was just...curiosity.

Hunkering in he searched through file after file waiting for something to strike him. Catheri said Phonm's hidden storage room was full of childhood junk, but his computers were full of Sethren Company data. There had to be something, and eventually he found it.

"Well, this is interesting," Taylor mused, his neck stiff from the chair.

The data under this section of files was empty, only the file names were there. Files like *SpecTech4.1*, and *RecovFileJohnS*, and *R34dM3T4ylor*. Taylor leaned back in his seat. As if on cue, a file fell from his desk. It was the suspect file Keeb handed him earlier, with all this Phonm business Taylor had almost forgotten about it.

"What the..." Taylor looked down at a note Keeb had left in the file. It was Keeb's handwriting:

'Taylor's suspect. Hopefully he won't fuck it up'

Did Keeb really leave himself notes? Did he have *no* confidence in Taylor? Taylor wasn't sure why, but something really bothered him about this. He picked up the file. He read Keeb's note again, and crumpled it. He imagined Keeb intended to remove that note before giving the file to Taylor. Well, Keeb was going to learn something about Taylor today. A pissed off Taylor was a bad Taylor to have around.

"Okay Keeb. I'll be sure not to fuck it up," he said out loud. *Better not to take any chances*, Taylor smirked to himself. To do so would be irresponsible. Taylor turned from the Spec7 and grabbed his desk phone to call dispatch. Truth be told, he almost forgot to make the arrest today. That didn't mean Keeb was right though.

"Communications...," answered dispatch. No enthusiasm there.

"It's me," he said, as if they would know who he was, as if they waited by the phone just for him to call. "Assemble the Duty Squad in the YARD, ready in five minutes," he said and disconnected without a reply. Using the Duty Squad to arrest someone would certainly piss Keeb off. And it should be a lot of fun. As he gathered himself from the desk Taylor tried to remember who the Squad Head on duty was, if it was Lanway with his meticulously polished gear and charm, Kellick and his career stalling brutality, or stubby Tanner with his endless marriage jokes. Taylor actually liked the jokes. He hoped it was Tanner, he could use a laugh.

He shut the Spec7 briefcase and slid it inconspicuously underneath his desk. No one would snoop through his office, but he made sure it was hidden anyways. Even under his desk it felt too exposed. He should have a safe box for such things. He made a mental note to have maintenance install one. Keeb wouldn't be working this late, he should be home by now. Taylor hustled through the absent hallway and left the precinct. He crossed the street to the Yard where the Squad was assembling. He wasn't about to let Keeb's suspect get away, the Squad would make sure of that. Street lights brightened the way. A sandpaper voice grated through the hustle and bustle of New Seattle City's evening chatter.

Kellick. He should have known. Kellick's voice dominated the YARD as Taylor approached. "MOVE you nasty things! Gleason, where's your Kevlar? Secure that gear!!" Kellick gave orders with a voice like a dentist's old drill. He sounded like he had screamed himself hoarse from the age of ten.

People felt uncomfortable around Kellick; Taylor admired that. Kellick was crude and unrefined, and he made no attempts to hide that. Taylor had never worked with him until now. To hell with Tanner and his dumb jokes, hearing Kellick's voice reminded him fondly of the Academy.

"Kellick, nicely done. Here," Taylor handed him the file. Crisp blue eyes stared down at Taylor, file in hand.

"His name is…" Taylor paused, having forgotten the name already, "…Aaron Mott, a very dangerous target. A suspected serial killer… oops. I've said too much."

Kellick stood with his head imperceptibly cocked to the side. "You called us to help you arrest someone? Have you lost your mind? We are heavy tactical support, not babysitters," Kellick said.

"This is a very high profile case, Commander Keeb doesn't want to take any chances," Taylor said further. Really it was a compliment, but Kellick didn't seem flattered. The Duty Squad was fit for tackling anything short of a war. Taylor jolted when an unexpected voice spoke from behind him.

"Did I really say that?" He knew Keeb's voice. Everyone in Precinct Four did.

Squad Head Kellick snapped his feet together with a crisp salute. "Good evening, Commander," Kellick said.

"At ease," Commander Keeb replied. Kellick stood at rest with his hands crossed behind his back and feet shoulder length apart. *How much has he heard?* Taylor wondered. Suddenly his little stunt felt ill advised. Too late now… Taylor turned to face him.

"Is this too much? It seemed like a situation worth putting everything into," Taylor said. His tone was sincere, but Keeb knew him too well for that.

"Detective Taylor," he almost hissed as he said it. Keeb's face burned red. "What the hell are you doing?" he gritted his teeth as he spoke.

"Sir, I'm just following your orders, sir."

"Orders?!" Keeb warned.

"I'm sorry sir, but you said this guy is our suspect," Taylor began. "A serial killer like this, and I know it's only my second day on the job, but I didn't think we should take any chances," Taylor said. Keeb had clenched his jaw so tight Taylor thought he heard a tooth snap. Keeb was trapped, forced into play, and he knew it. If he ordered the Duty Squad to stand down now, and then something did go wrong, it would be blamed on him.

"I don't care who--" Keeb stopped himself, took a breath, and as if nothing was ever wrong continued in an entirely new voice. "Well this is one way to get your man. Overkill, but surely effective. Have it your way, Detective."

It scared Taylor. One minute Keeb was ready to tear Taylor's head off and the next minute he was encouraging him. With a near smile Keeb turned and left. Taylor gaped. Keeb's sudden change of heart was entirely unexpected. And what was he *about* to say? Taylor buzzed with adrenaline. With his thoughts tumbling, Taylor approached the Crawler where the SQUAD was assembling. Rose saw him coming.

"You called us to arrest someone for you? Maybe we should be on vandalism and graffiti watch next," Rose joked, tossing a look to his buddy Gleason. It was a slight insult to openly criticize Taylor, but more importantly Rose should have addressed him by his title.

"You aren't nervous, are you Rose?" Taylor replied, still shaking Keeb from his head.

Rose's smirk disappeared in a drop. "Pretty sure we can handle it," he snarled.

"Quick turnaround on this murder, I heard about it this morning. Must be easy when you don't have to worry about evidence, right?" Gleason taunted him next. Taylor remembered he applied for Detective as well. His first name was…Joe? Nah, that's not it.

"Keep trying Gleason, one day you might make Detective too," Taylor smiled, speaking loud enough for all to hear. In mid-motion Gleason snapped to attention as Squad Head Kellick appeared.

"Why am I still waiting on you, Gleason??" Kellick spat. Gleason scrambled into the Crawler as if his life depended on it. He didn't want Kellick's personal attention in any way. Kellick motioned to fire the engines.

Kellick, Rose, Gleason, and three females comprised the squad on duty. Women cops were competitive, edgy, and pushed themselves harder than any of the male cops. And there was no quicker way to get action than volunteering for Squad Duty. Taylor only knew Officer Bell; the other two females were new recruits. Bell was a veteran, an adrenaline junky who volunteered for everything dangerous. She looked like she pissed standing up. She actually had two prosthetic fingers, lost in a knife fight during an arrest. Guy pulled a blade on her, it was either her fingers or her neck. Poor guy never made it back to prison.

The Crawler growled to life. It rode on six axled wheels to navigate any terrain and was plated with seven centimeters of poly armor. Taylor knew it also crushed street signs. A dozen eyes from Precinct Four watched it go, eager to hear the tales upon its return.

||Chapter 9||

The rear of the Crawler was large and divided into two compartments, and Taylor occupied his half in solace. He heard the crew on the other side working each other up. It was such a joke to them. He couldn't help but feel the smallest remorse for the suspect, Aaron Mott. The fact that he felt anything meant he needed a vacation. "Screw the guy." Aaron Mott wasn't innocent. No one was.

The drive to the harbor lasted only minutes. He knew the building was near when the smell of seaweed burned his nose. He knew the location–an old amusement aquarium that bred and sold exotic fish. Aaron Mott was a retail shift supervisor according to the file. More and more Taylor knew Mott wasn't the killer, his detective instincts told him so. Killers just didn't work late shifts at pet stores.

That didn't stop Taylor. Mott was guilty of something, somewhere, especially if Keeb named him. Taylor made a final review of the arrest file, flipping to the employment history. There was a short gig with the police department as a clerk, a decade ago. What were the odds of that?

The Crawler lurched, sending Taylor into the wall. Kellick's voice roared about running someone's ass over next time. Not much longer now. Soon Mott would be under arrest. Taylor flipped through the file out of habit. It was getting darker, but the good Citizens of New Seattle City were still shopping. *We're stopped...*

Taylor heard doors of the Crawler open. Bell and Gleason shouted commands, and like a wave the Squad dismounted and took cover in position outside the exotic fish store. An elderly couple quickly turned and hustled away, dragging a walker with them. Kellick walked to the door, armored and without a helmet. He famously refused to wear a helmet, believing he was invincible until his time was up. When asked about the armor plating he did wear, Kellick simply answered that it was comfortable. Flanked by the team, Kellick kicked open the glass door to the exotic aquarium, the squad stormed inside. It really was overkill, Taylor imagined he was weaving quite a reputation if this was how he operated two days into his new position.

"POLICE!! ON THE GROUND!!"

Taylor strolled in, he figured his casual demeanor would help lessen the anxiety of the civilians inside, and he typically felt at ease when everyone else was panicking. He entered just in time to see Bell leap across the counter and snatch the register clerk, pinning his face to the countertop with her rifle. A customer near the golden piranha tank was tripped to the ground by Rose and held there under Rose's boot. Not to be outdone the smaller of the female recruits grabbed the sales floor clerk by his hair and slammed his nose into the counter.

"Everyone stay calm, I'm Detective Taylor of Precinct Four, I'm looking for Aaron Mott," he said as officially as he could. No doubt Taylor would hear a door open or a window and have to chase someone into the harbor.

"I'm Aaron," came a very timid, very nervous voice.

A small and terrified man, Keeb's age, walked slowly out from the narrow hallway behind the reception counter. Taylor almost rolled his eyes. If he didn't know it before, he knew it for certain now, this was not a vicious serial killer. No sooner did Aaron present himself than Kellick slammed him against the wall, pinning the length of his rifle against his neck. Mott's face turned purple, his neck contorted and ready to snap. Taylor looked away. *Why did he pick you, Aaron?*

Just like that it was done. Rose took his boot off the customer and helped escort Mott outside. Bell slid back over the countertop again, giving a glare that dared anyone to look her in the eye. "Squad, thank these good Citizens for their cooperation," Taylor said. The man with the broken nose whimpered on the ground. He knew better than to speak, his personal rights went as far as the courthouse documents they were printed on. Taylor turned to go, following the other female recruit. Once outside Gleason jumped into a giddy play by play. Bell laughed about how Mott's face turned purple. Kellick said nothing. Taylor jumped when he saw reporters were waiting near the Crawler.

"Mott! Did you know your victims? What do you have to say for yourself?"

Taylor almost choked. The Crawler attracted media attention, that was true, but only Keeb, Taylor, and Kellick knew the suspect's name.

"I haven't done anything," Mott said to the eager camera crew. Another media van sped down the street. How did this get so public? Taylor let Mott climb into the rear of the Crawler.

"Get ready, there they go!" The guise of control masked Commander Keeb's worry.

"Kellick, ha! That guy doesn't waste time... Poor bastards," the other man scoffed, readying a rocket.

"Too bad it's Kellick. I would have preferred killing Lanway," Commander Keeb said.

"Yeah, you sound real torn up about it."

"Are you sure this will work? The poly armor plating is military grade..."

"I'm damn sure. I just need one clear shot. And Keeb..." the assassin said, rubbing his trigger finger on his chin.

Keeb waited for him to speak. He swore he felt the building sway from this high up, the wind through the broken windows didn't help. Keeb already knew what the man was about to say, the sooner this was over with the better.

"Jack *will* find out that you killed Taylor, is that going to be a problem?"

"To hell with Jack Sethren." And he meant it. Taylor was a punk and he crossed the line for the last time, activating the Duty Squad was a direct insult. Keeb wasn't going to let Taylor get away with it this time, even if Jack Sethren was protecting him. Jack Sethren could kiss his ass, Keeb was not a puppet.

Taylor was interrogating his suspect inside the back of the Crawler. He tried to ignore the laughter coming through the divider wall. "Aaron Mott, let's talk about the murders of Ellen Ngu and Kayd L. Jr., not to mention torture and unlawful entry," Taylor said. He had almost forgotten to surrender his blaster before the doors closed, a rookie mistake with a prisoner. Rose had kindly reminded him.

"I never hurt them," Aaron said.

"I was expecting you to say, 'wasn't me'."

"I've never hurt anybody."

"Mr. Mott, we have evidence and a motive, and with your record…" Taylor paused, realizing he was on autopilot. Mott had no record.

"We have everything we need for a conviction." Liar liar. Taylor was in new territory. He'd condemned criminals for crimes they weren't guilty of, but they were always guilty of something, so it never bothered him before. But what he was doing now seemed unfair to Taylor, *unfair* being a word he didn't believe in.

"You've got the wrong guy," Aaron said.

"Where were you last night?" Taylor threw down a picture of Ellen Ngu. Aaron's face turned away.

"Home, with my wife."

"Try again," Taylor said. There was no way Mott was the killer, but this was Keeb's roadmap, Taylor was just following it. Most likely Aaron could be free after six months in jail, after Keeb felt satisfied for whatever he was holding a grudge about. And in the meantime the real killer would have a change of heart and abandon his evil ways, while Taylor perfected his martini. That would be the best thing for Taylor and for the killer, then everyone would be happy.

The Crawler lurched to the side as it went over a curb.

"Ellen Ngu. She's hardly recognizable," Taylor slapped down another picture. Mott looked ill, Taylor knew he didn't recognize these photos. Aaron held his tongue, staring at the pictures.

Taylor flew from his seat, slamming into the wall.

An explosion flipped the Crawler onto its side, flinging Taylor and Aaron against the inside wall. Dazed, Taylor found himself looking up at the ceiling. Time stretched and his ears rang. He reached down for his blaster but realized he had surrendered it. A second defeaning blast split the Crawler in two. The front half of the Crawler disintegrated in flesh and steel. Smoke billowed from inside the cabin. Taylor instinctively grabbed Aaron by his shoulders and dragged him, half aware of the searing pieces of shrapnel.

Taylor yanked and tugged Mott away from the remaining pieces of the Crawler, ignoring the burns on his hand. Mott's heel drew a crooked trail of blood.

]]Chapter 10[[

Ten years prior to Taylor's unjust Detective promotion, ten years before the Crawler was blown up with Taylor inside of it, something sinister was occurring in the privacy of the Sethren Company Labs. The real John was dead, but in a twist of fate his personality was captured by a neurologically enhanced android. And thanks to John's intense hallucinations, a second android programmed itself to be his daughter. Through a sick twist of fate however, they fell into Jack Sethren's hands. They were captured the moment Cargo Lock Five landed on Earth. At the hands of the man responsible, John's vengeance was forced to wait.

Temperature 14.3 C. Time 1136:02. Self check engaged. Neural map online. Warning: Cache load exceeds limits. Subroutine systems: user 1, local. Visual Readout display 1.1, adjustment for low light: Go infrared. Self operational checks status: neural code retained. Position: unknown. Download File: ... ...download complete. My daughter... ERROR RUN BIOS vs. 2.2 rebooting...waiting...reboot complete.

Name: ... Name...timeout error. Completed download. Name:...John. Humanoid Neural Tech Model: 1.0 download complete. Install drivers: corrupted files...attempting Master Reset...loading...loading...

"The download is complete, Mr. Sethren, and the original memories were kept intact," Felix said unplugging the data cable from John and from John's *'daughter'*.

"It's amazing, this technology," Jack Sethren said, speaking for once.

Felix was in awe as well, but mostly from the second android, the *daughter*. John's android made sense, considering the incredibly unusual circumstances that allowed him to happen. But the *daughter*, she manifested from nothing more than the *living John's* thoughts. That was something completely unexpected.

Felix was amazed the androids onboard CPU didn't burn out. And he was surprised that *both* androids didn't become John. Felix craved the chance to study it all, analyze how it happened, even if it took years. Only occasionally did he stop to think how John was a real man who died under terrible circumstances.

"John died mentally unstable, no surprise there. The 'daughter' android sort of appeared from John's hallucinations. I've never seen anything like it," Felix added with a glow. It was scientifically incredible.

"You said the new programs are uploaded in 'John' now?" Jack Sethren asked. He had kept the oddest look during this entire discovery, as if he had something planned that just tickled him.

"Yes sir."

"Then let 'em loose," Jack Sethren ordered. Felix objected, in silence of course. For a thousand reasons he could not imagine releasing these two machines. Most of all as a scientist he wanted this technology to stay with him. He picked the reason that might appeal best to Jack Sethren.

"But... John wants to kill you, and this *machine* thinks it is John."

Jack Sethren pretended to contemplate. "Well, that's fair. After all, I did kill everyone onboard Space Station Hephaestus, those poor souls deserve a chance to get even," Jack smiled. Felix hated when Jack Sethren mocked the dead. "Besides, John will now hunt the others first, and when my former Elites begin disappearing, I'll know to be prepared."

"Excuse me, Mr. Sethren? I'm so sorry to interrupt," said Jack's assistant, Kita, who had entered the room. She appeared like a ghost, an impressive feat in pointed heels. Kita was a protégé. Felix had hoped Jack meant to make use of her aptitudes in science, instead he relegated her to an assistant. For whatever reason, Jack Sethren never let Kita near the old sciences. He never let anyone near them, pretending they didn't exist, letting the world think they didn't exist…. Oh the old sciences certainly did exist, Felix was proof.

"What is it, Kita?" Jack Sethren turned to her.

"Mayor Bloom is here, he wants to go over plans for the construction of Sethren Tower," she said.

"Construction is two years from now. Reschedule," Jack Sethren ordered. Kita left without another word, Jack succumbed to another self satisfying smile. Sethren Company was finally taking shape, his empire grew by the day. *By the hour.* And in a half decade he would command the city with a sky scraper like no other. His Sethren Tower, once built, would become New Seattle City's greatest icon, forging the fate of history to come.

"Jack, *we* found these machines, think of what we can learn!"

Jack said nothing. Felix may as well have been alone in the room at this point, fondling a look of frustration as Jack Sethren left.

Felix could not lift his gaze from the floor. Survival had aligned him to Jack, but that was long ago. Why was Jack Sethren doing this?

The sick irony of it all was that John died because of Jack Sethren. If you have to kill a man, kill him. But let all of him die, don't torment his soul. Felix never forgave himself for what occurred on that Space Station, and now the ghosts of Hephaestus would haunt him even more.

Felix had acted out of loyalty, a loyalty that was dying ever so slowly. He had never questioned Jack Sethren before, but he couldn't help himself anymore. Jack suffered a fascination that Felix had yet to decipher. Jack Sethren was obsessed with someone, to the point that he had collected thousands of hours of video surveillance from schools, stores, hotels, even an orphanage. He never explained what he was looking for, but whatever it was pushed Jack Sethren with more passion, or contempt, than Felix had ever seen on the man.

And if there was another reason for Felix's suffering loyalty, it would be the room he had found. There was something Felix had discovered, something utterly disturbing. It was Jack Sethren's most unexplainable whim to date; the clones. Illegal under every political entity, Jack Sethren had a series of clones constructed based on the DNA of a single man. It wasn't *who* this man was that bothered Felix. It's *what* Jack did to the clones.

He killed them, in every imagineable way.

One night not long ago Felix had been drawn to the sounds of weeping. He followed the noise to just outside Jack's private room. It was Jack's voice, sobbing like a child. Felix, risking everything, hid down the hallway in a storage closet until Jack left. He sneaked inside Jack's private room.

A mangled body lay sprawled on the floor. The body belonged to one of the clones, bludgeoned to death with a steel pipe. As Felix stared in horror he noticed a slew of weapons and torture devices... No one knew of that room except Felix. He wished more than anything he did not know.

Lastly, Felix knew of one clone that was made differently. Jack let this clone live, though the life he condemned it to was no gift or act of kindness. This one clone had been engineered as a baby. Jack ordered it to be placed in an orphanage. A fate worse than death by the reputation orphanages had, Jack had constant contact with the director of the orphanage. He could have provided everything for that boy. What was the name they gave him? Taylor? Poor lad. Just another one of Jack's special projects.

But that was then. After ten years, just as they were
programmed to, the androids began to act on their own
finally. Today, John's vengeance was getting what it
deserved. One by one, he was finally making them all pay.
The next Elite to suffer was Roth, but he was different, he
didn't have any family. A true soldier at heart, he found
himself on the battlefield too often to form any sort of
important relationship. If he had kids, he didn't know them.
That was not to say that Roth was without feelings, because
he actually loved someone very much. He was only human,
and his affections had to go somewhere. Roth loved a
whore, her name was Sallee. John found her, and they were
both suffering right now.

        "Please don't do this," Roth cried. Sallee's
quivering betrayed her otherwise stony face. But she wasn't
as brave as she let on. John knew that, he read her emotions
as easily as a book and with more detail. The blade always
brought out the fear. John looked to Sallee. He did not
enjoy causing pain, but vengeance knows no joy.
        "You're the best Roth has. No kids, no family. Just
her," John said. An entertainment screen reflected a soft
light off of John.
        "Let her go, please, take me!" Roth pleaded, barely
able to contain himself. John felt the emotions through his
sensors.
        "It doesn't work that way," John said.
        Roth's breath steadied. "Please," Sallee begged.
Roth said nothing.
        "I hoped you had more than just her. A son, a
daughter, but you only love her. Can you kill her, to protect
her?"
        The light shifted and Roth caught a closer look at
John. Roth thought his eyes had been playing tricks on him,

but there was no mistake now. This man was not human, up close he was like an unfinished mannequin. "What are you?" Roth asked.

John waited motionless.

"She has nothing to do with anything. I did those things, let me take her place," Roth begged, his eyes full of defeat.

John would not delay any longer. "Do you choose to let me kill her?" John asked. He could not be bargained with, but Roth had to try. Everyone had to try. John sensed a change in Roth, but it wasn't the change he was expecting. In fact, John had a very hard time reading Roth right now, as if he was shielding his thoughts, his emotions.

"I'll do it," Roth said and held out an unwavering hand. When John looked Roth in the eyes, oddly, he sensed nothing. A self diagnostic showed that his sensors were still functioning, there must be some unusual pattern in Roth's thought processes that John could not detect. Usually, when John looked someone in the eye, he sensed many layers of fear. Roth was not displaying any emotion. John stepped forward, handing him the blade. Before the blade even rested in Roth's palm he sensed its familiarity. He had used many blades, and he was surprised how his muscles became excited by its grip. He knew with precision which arteries to pierce, how to slip past bones, how to stifle a scream. Roth held the knife. He had not held a blade for decades. Ironic, Roth thought, how his hand was so happy to wield it, considering what he was about to do. He looked one last time at Sallee. He never expected to be free of the things he had done, but there was a time that he had hoped. There was a time that he had thought he might live a normal life with a girl and settle down. Sallee might have been that girl, if ever there was a girl. There was one thing about Roth, however, that made it hard for him to ever do the right thing. It was his selfishness. "Sallee, I'm sorry," he whispered. Roth lifted the tip of the blade over his left chest and thrust the point into his own heart.

"NOOO!!" John screamed. He slammed Roth's body through the wall, bursting plaster and mortar. Sallee shrieked, flailing against her restraints. Darkness wrapped itself around John's unstable CPU. His mechanical screams echoed for hours.

Taylor's paid leave was short, a mere three days lost in a drunken coma. Somewhere amidst the rising pillars of smoke from scattered Crawler parts he remembered thinking he was dead. Vina had left him. More precisely she kicked him out. He came home from the hospital, bandaged and aching, to find his belongings on the front porch. Those boxes were probably still there. He was surprised she had it in her. In a way he was happy for Vina, not that divorce did her any favors. But she was free of him, and that was good for her. Ironically, now he missed her.

Taylor decided that since the Crawler attack didn't kill him, whisky might. So for three days he drank. He came to the precinct long enough to use the shower and change his clothes, and in very sparse moments to check on his investigation without Keeb knowing. Ever since the Crawler attack, Taylor felt a sort of commitment to his duties as a Detective, which was where the whisky came in. Taylor usually didn't care about anything, so when he did feel something, he didn't know what to do with himself. With Aaron Mott's death, and with his own near death experience, Taylor had really *felt* something. Taylor decided to scheme a way into getting his sick leave terminated so he could get back to work. Coincidentally, Keeb ended it for him. There was another murder, if you could call it that. Hell on earth was another name for it.

It wasn't like anything he had ever seen. Taylor was staring at hatred unleashed. Two victims, a man and a prostitute. Neither one worked for Sethren Company, which hurt his connection theory. Taylor's delicate state notwithstanding Keeb had brought in another detective, Silas Maheny, to 'help' Taylor. This murder/suicide had occurred the same day as the Crawler attack, but was only discovered days later by a concerned neighbor. The smell made Taylor weave to the side momentarily. He caught himself before Keeb or Silas noticed.

Keeb had not looked at Taylor once since his arrival. He and Silas maintained safe working distance near the hole in the wall where Roth's body was found. It almost seemed like Keeb didn't want him there, so what was the point of ending Taylor's leave? Taylor wasn't going to receive a cold shoulder from afar, he approached without invitation. Aaron Mott deserved some amount of justice, something that wasn't going to happen unless Taylor made it happen. It was time to remind everyone this was *his* case.

"So someone killed Aaron Mott before he could clear his name," Taylor blurted. He could have sugar coated it. They finally lifted their heads pretending to see Taylor for the first time. Keeb and Silas exchanged the briefest of looks.

"Taylor. Good to meet you," Silas said with a warm handshake, cold on the inside.

Taylor held the shake firm and looked him dead in the eyes.

"Right. This is likely a copycat killer, it's a crazy world out there," Silas chimed. Taylor rubbed his nose. Silas was clearly brought on board to steer the investigation in Keeb's favor should Taylor fail. Taylor hated that.

"And as far as the Crawler attack goes, terrorist groups are a constant threat," Silas added. There it was, everything wrapped with a nice shiny bow. Taylor had done the same thing many times. This was giving him a headache. Who *did* blow up the Crawler? He couldn't believe it was just an opportunistic attack.

"Taylor, after you review the evidence, you'll agree with Detective Maheny," Commander Keeb stated. Taylor knew what he was supposed to say in return. Agreeing with Keeb was rule number one in the police manual.

"Don't count on that, Commander. I never felt Aaron Mott was a legitimate suspect. I'm going to find the real killer, and I'm going to arrest them," Taylor said. He stopped for a moment and waited. Taylor had just insulted Keeb on many levels, among them, getting an innocent man killed. But Keeb's short temper never surfaced, instead he just smiled reluctantly at Taylor.

"You just need some time to remember how things work around here," Keeb said while leaving. By the time Taylor cleared his throat Keeb was gone. He looked over at Silas feigning a casual pose, smiling like a teenager.

"Maybe our victim here killed the prostitute and then ended his own life, knife to the chest," Silas said. The nonsense burned.

"Yes, and naturally he then threw himself through the wall," Taylor added. Silas did not reply, instead he nursed a look of analysis. Taylor's instincts said that Silas was not as dumb as he pretended. Either way Silas fell content to study the adjacent room on his own. Taylor surveyed the room again, when his stomach stopped turning from the sight of it.

"It's just blood, and…stuff," Taylor said to himself, trying not to vomit. When he had his bearings he surveyed the room a little more. He couldn't buy the copycat theory, same as he couldn't buy Aaron Mott as the killer. A copycat would be more like the other kills, and there were differences here. The previous murders were controlled, like a well executed plan. Two victims, one of them was alive, one was dead. Clean. Deliberate. This room also had two victims, but the similarities died with them. This was emotional, a dark canvas painted with rage. Something pushed the killer past his point. Right now Taylor wasn't sure if this was related to Phonm or Kayd, but he did know that a human couldn't have caused this much destruction. The crazy cyborg statement from Phonm suddenly felt like it might be true.

Taylor sniffed a timeline; when *could* Roth have killed himself? An emotional killer wouldn't have let him. He must have killed himself first, before the killer became unstable. And since Roth's suicide was not part of the plan, the killer lost it. The killer imploded, knocked Roth through the wall. With Roth already dead, the prostitute was the only thing left for his rage. Her cause of death could be described many ways. The most recognizable part of her was the skin of her face, peeled halfway from the skull. The rest of her was all over the place; torn, mangled, cut, ripped, splattered seemingly everywhere. Bone fragments, intestine, hair, tips of a finger, a toe... CSD would spend days trying to document body parts and types of blood splatter and still have a fraction of what happened. Taylor weaved to the side again. This room would haunt him for the rest of his life.

"So what do you think happened here?" Silas asked, returning out of nowhere. He wasn't phased.

"Something bad," Taylor managed to say with his eyes pinned to a bloodless patch on the floor, clutching his bearings.

Silas leaned closer to Taylor with a whisper. "Wrong. You see a copycat, get it?" Silas said. It wasn't a question.

"No, I don't get it," Taylor said.

"Did you suddenly sprout a conscious? If Keeb wanted a real Detective, he would have promoted a *real* Detective, read me?" Silas unintentionally spat in Taylor's ear while he spoke.

Taylor's bearings came back. Now the room did not disturb him. Anger was a great anti nausea medicine. Taylor would not be controlled, and he certainly would not be threatened by this punk Silas. He had his own ideas about what happened here, and he was going to follow them. This was not a copycat, this was something else. Maybe it was the same killer and something went wrong, or maybe this was totally unrelated. But Taylor wasn't going to be led by Keeb anymore. Whatever change occurred after the Crawler attack Taylor didn't know, but he wasn't going to take it anymore. If Roth was connected to the others, Taylor would find how, because that was his job. And Silas would pay for spitting in his ear.

"You sing copycat 'til your nuts fall off. I'm finding the killer." Taylor turned to face Silas directly. "If you try to stop me... I'll ruin your perfect face." Taylor slapped Silas' shoulder, jolting him. It looked like a friendly gesture to the rest of the officers in the room, but Silas' wide eyed look proved he got the message.

Keeb and Silas couldn't cover this up. Sallee deserved justice.

]]Chapter 11[[

0346 hrs on day 11,014. I reminisced. After the intense emotional outbursts of Roth and Sallee I needed to let my neural sensors rest. I thought back to being trapped inside Cargo Lock Five. After floating through space for many years, finally, a salvage crew had found us. They towed us back to Earth. No one knew we were inside, they just wanted to sell the space junk they discovered. We were placed in a large storage bay for seven days after reentry to Earth. By the time they came to examine what they found we had already escaped.

Earth. The odds are incalculable, yet here we are. I realized then it was destiny, so I went to work right away. My vengeance had waited long enough. Finding the Elites took time. Roth was the third, but I found him. Then it hit me; thirty years? Without food? In freezing temperatures? How am I alive? Host Error…offline reboot…run/exec.bat… not again….

Taylor worked in his office long enough for the clock repeat itself. Catheri had brought him food and bottled water, which he barely touched. The Spec7 and Taylor were inseparable. He poured over the stolen data, examining every detail. If there was a link between Kayd, Phonm, and Roth, he was going to find it. Roth was the wildcard; he didn't work for the Sethren Company at all. The only thing about Roth's file was how there was so little in it. It might be nothing. Records were spotty in the years after the war ended.

Vina stopped by while Taylor was working but he didn't know it until after she left. She left some papers with

Catheri who doubtless was hearing her own wedding bells. Taylor didn't deserve Vin anyway, never did. He didn't deserve anyone. Taylor turned back to the files of nonsense.

So he wasn't a real detective, Keeb had promoted a puppet. *We'll see.* As he thumbed through screen after screen Taylor kept seeing Liberty Allegiance, a research organization. Taylor scratched his head. He wouldnt bother checking departmental databases to find Liberty Allegiance.

When political grounds began to stabilize, names changed, organizational purposes were quickly swapped. Liberty Allegiance reeked of something foul. Taylor tapped the desk. He remembered this name. Many of the Elites from the UMA found a home in Liberty Allegiance when the wars ended. But what would that have to do with anything? The wars were over, the Elites were irrelevant, weren't they? Kayd had that neck scar, and he was about the right age to have been an Elite. All of them were the right age, come to think of it.

'BLIP'

The Spec7 had made a noise. Taylor's chest tightened. The computer screen of the Spec7 actively blinked a dialogue box. Someone wanted to talk to him? This was impossible.

'BLIP'

Taylor scooted away from his desk and stepped back. How could someone hack into the Spec7? Taylor popped open the door to Catheri's empty office. He pulled the shades away to look outside at people enduring the wet streets under nightfall. New Seattle City never slept. If someone was watching Taylor's office, they were easily hidden. Taylor ran a crude diagnostic on the briefcase, the line seemed to be secure. Taylor couldn't force himself away, and one thought encouraged him. This was contact, communication. He wasn't in danger, at least not from this little blip. If he actually were in any danger, he wouldn't get a chat, he'd just be dead. Taylor held his anticipations in his chest as he reached an uncertain finger to the keyboard and activated the blip.

"You have very dangerous files. What are you looking for?"

"Ah, wh- what files?" Taylor replied, speaking into the Spec7.

"You don't have all day. Here's a clue: look for Cargo Lock Five."

::This session is ended::

Taylor leaned away from the briefcase. He stared at it, wondering if it would go off again. And then he laughed. "*Ah, wh-what files?!* Really??" Taylor couldn't believe that was all he managed to say. He receives a random, hacked message in the middle of the night, someone who may know something about his case, and all he says is that? Taylor could only imagine the person on the other end of that call, scratching their head, wondering how Taylor made it to Detective. Well, at least Taylor knew enough to not put too much weight into anonymous tips. It was another way of being led, and it was a good way of getting killed. What reasons would someone have to contact him like this? And who would even have the resources to do it?

After a few hours the clock read ridiculously late. Catheri was at home. Vina was at home. Taylor was working. Strange computers were talking to him. He thought of Ayne, for whatever reason. Seeing her reopened a door in his memory. Taylor flicked his fingers on the desk for good measure. She might be downtown right now. He really could use a break before anything else weird happened, but, and against his usual self, he stayed and worked. This wasn't like him, all work and no play. He didn't know this new Taylor. He wondered how long he would last.

Jack Sethren gazed out the windows. The City sprawled beneath him. His room claimed the top five floors of Sethren Tower. He stood there, like the eye of God, watching. Jack Sethren placed a hand on the wall of reinforced glass. As impressive as his view was, he couldn't help but be distracted. Some of the surviving Elites had contacted him about Kayd, Phonm, and now Roth. They wanted to go to war, they wanted Jack to pool his resources and track down this assassin. The cowards, they were afraid. Jack Sethren was disappointed in his once notorious unit, there was a time that they were invincible. Still, he didn't need them ruining his plans, so he assured his brethren that there would be an internal investigation, and that the assassin would be found and punished. But Jack already knew who, or actually what, killed them.

The androids were to blame, mostly. He could have stopped them of course, but he was using them for his plans with Taylor. They had performed brilliantly, they were easily as efficient as his Elites had ever been. He missed his old squad but after the performance the androids gave he would choose them over his Elites any day. He never imagined what they were capable of when he released them, something Felix would remind him about when he mustered the resolve to contradict Jack Sethren. The 'John' android actually did all the work. He entered the Tower by scaling the walls. Then through air ducts, created a hole on the twenty-seventh floor, and entered undetected. Impressive.

The daughter android served a purpose, mostly in tracking down the Elites, and the two of them together were so unique. Jack Sethren just couldn't get over how the two androids actually thought they were real people. Jack Sethren never met the real John, he wondered how closely the android had replicated him. There were so many sciences and technologies that just couldn't survive the wars,

Jack Sethren had at least managed to preserve Felix, a brilliant move on his part. Not all of his plans worked out so well, of course.

   Keeb. Jack couldn't even think his name without wanting to spit out the taste, the Commander almost ruined a plan set in motion decades ago. Keeb should have known better, he had already failed him once, and after the way Jack Sethren had punished him, it should have been the last time. Yet with this new rash of incompetence, Jack Sethren was already preparing a new commander for Precinct Four. Not that he blamed Commander Keeb entirely, there was an old military philosophy about *'understanding the commander's intent'* at all times. Jack never conveyed his intent, ever, and it stood to reason that from time to time his orders would be misinterpreted.

   Despite the setbacks, despite Keeb almost killing Taylor, despite Taylor almost killing himself, his endgame was not compromised. In fact, it could be working out better than he had ever hoped. Taylor had become what Jack Sethren needed him to become. The androids were still performing their missions, thanks to Felix's subtle reprogramming. And Keeb's insufficiencies may have actually strengthened the showdown to come. Taylor just had to follow the trail of death to Jack Sethren's door.

   Catheri had barely sat down at her desk, ready to start a new day of work, when the phone rang. "Detective Taylor's office," Catheri answered the phone.

   "Cath, it's me," Taylor said. He needed something, she could tell in his voice.

   "Good morning, handsome," she smiled.

   "I need something."

   She rolled her eyes. It was difficult being right all

the time, though by now she should be used to it. "Oh? Does it come with breasts?" she joked, trying to be fun, but nervous at the same time. Taylor's requests were usually complicated. Whatever it was must be important, Taylor was never up before Catheri, and he was certainly never working before her.

"No. I need you to research documents from the old Space Port Shipping yards. Everything within the last ten... no… twenty years," he said. The manifests and records from the Space Port Shipping Co. were as organized as a junk drawer in a deserted landfill. "Just pull up anything titled Cargo Lock Five."

A name? That was at least something. There should only be a thousand or so containers bearing that number. Did he want the Port's own cargo, or just shipped units? And did he also want salvaged containers? Just a few of those details might keep her from spending a week on this. "Fine," she said. Taylor had already ended the call. She came close to uttering the word 'jerk', but she restrained herself. Catheri realized she was playing with her hair the whole time she was speaking to Taylor. As much as she hated him, she loved him twice as much. She jumped when she realized someone else was in the room.

"Excuse me, is Detective Taylor here?"

"He's not in yet," Catheri replied. She could smell cologne from across the room.

"When will he be here?" the man said, a look like he was the cock and walk all in one. Catheri hated that look. Only one man had ever pulled it off, and that man was Taylor.

"I wish I could say. I can take a message," she faked a smile. This man had a look that needed to be slapped off his face. Not punched, slapped. Catheri had a gift for slapping. And for spanking.

"Tell him Detective Silas was looking for him,"

Silas said.

It only took four and a half hours for Catheri to bring him records of everything named Cargo Lock Five. The woman was amazing. Spaceports, and space stations for that matter, had several ways of storing or shipping cargo and people. The best part was how meticulously detailed their records were, once you actually found what you were looking for. That was also the worst part, Taylor would spend hours trying to determine the value of that anonymous tip. But looking at these files reminded him, he had always wanted to travel in space himself, he hadn't thought of that consciously though for years, not since he was a teenager.

Too bad he couldn't have her point out which Cargo Lock 5 he wanted. There were hundreds of them, it was an incredibly generic number assignment that was used over and over. Taylor tapped his finger on the table. If his mystery contact was on to something, then this cargo lock or container or whatever it was became a piece of the puzzle. If not, Taylor was wasting time. There were so many shipping manifests that wouldn't even be truthful; smuggled religious books, political propaganda, weapons, stowaways, deserters, etc. How would he know the clue he was looking for was declared on these documents?

Taylor set the files aside and collapsed against the back of his seat. This *real work* business was exhausting. Earlier when Catheri brought him the files she had set them across his lap, a teasing caress before going back to her desk in the other room. Instead of being aroused Taylor sensed her insecurity. He didn't always understand women. Did she need a quickie after doing all that work? He hadn't shown her much attention lately, and he sensed it affecting her self esteem. Which, ironically, made him want her less.

Taylor's office had been choking him long enough, it was time for air. He got up and brushed his pants down, a habitual exercise after standing. He bypassed the hallway and the people in it without really noticing anyone or anything, somewhere he realized it was getting close to lunchtime, but he wasn't hungry yet. His eyes were open but he walked in a daze, he had stayed up all night. His mind was scrubbed. When he stepped outside he had to shield his eyes, sunlight was the last thing he needed. Taylor winced from the light, but before he had time to retreat back inside, before he had time to even think about what to do next, something gushed down on him. Cold, heavy, and wet. Red paint had splashed down on Taylor, liters of it. He tried to wipe his eyes, instead smearing the paint across his face. When he finally could see he noticed a bucket on a windowsill above the door, tipped over like some fucking childhood prank. Fucking seriously? The break room window slammed shut with laughter. He hated being laughed at.

"Fuck!" Taylor screamed. He wiped and wiped his face but the paint lolled down his head. It was cold and thick, molesting every crevice and fold of skin. He felt it go down his back and under his belt. Taylor was furious, and hurt. He hadn't felt like this in a very, very long time. A prank. A fucking prank. Fuck them! Who the fuck did they think they were!! Taylor could have done anything in that moment. If he had his gun on him, someone would have died. Taylor didn't need this shit.

Taylor stormed back inside. He had to get control of himself. He knew this feeling, this embarrassment, and the rage that followed, and he knew he needed to contain it. A fresh silence moistened the air, nobody was willing to make a sound at the sight of Taylor. Crossing the lobby he left a dripping trail of red paint behind him. He had never felt so many eyes on him, not since he was a boy. The paint burned his nose. In the back of his mind he wondered why he was surprised. He shouldn't be, he should have anticipated some kind of idiotic prank or hazing. There was a cold air around him ever since the Crawler attack, only Taylor survived while several other good cops died. Taylor survived, and he knew something would happen. But this was fucked up. And yet it *worked*. They couldn't have torn him apart any better.

Taylor stomped, the sound of paint sloshing between his legs, and entered the shower room at the end of the hallway. He walked in fully clothed and hit the water. Some other fuckhead could clean up the paint on the ground, fuck them. The warm water was comforting, he sprayed it bluntly into his eyes, hoping they would stop burning. Sons of bitches. He needed that shower, needed it like a scared child, which burned more than the laughter. Paint poured endlessly down the drain. Seeing paint wash away made Taylor feel the slightest, tiniest bit better. So many hateful thoughts and emotions bubbled and poured through him, but he wanted to just let them go. He wasn't a child anymore. It wasn't like before. He could protect himself now. This was just a stupid prank. Taylor stayed in the shower until his fingertips looked like raisins, and then he stayed a little longer. His clothes weighed a ton, but he didn't care. Let the water wash it all away. Eventually Taylor stepped out, sopping wet and still fully clothed, and he went to his locker. Water pooled at his shoes, his feet slipping a little inside of them. He would find a new suit inside. Opening his locker door he slammed it shut immediately. Someone had splashed red paint on all of his suits.

"Fucking shit!! You fucks!!" Taylor burst and punched his locker. No one was watching Taylor, they were afraid to, but he didn't know that. He felt every invisible eye, and he couldn't take it. He pounded his locker until it came off the wall and then he stomped on it until his terrible fit subsided. All of his shirts were ruined. Heat poured out of his neck and face, he had really worked himself up that time. He felt better, however. He had a bursting point, and they found it. But now that his locker rested in bent metal pieces, he felt a little better. Taylor took in a long breath and realized his knuckles were throbbing, and the big right knuckle was bleeding. It felt good to bleed right now. Taylor took another breath and decided to get dressed. He intended to take someone else's clothes and they could fuck off if they had a problem with it. A new nameplate caught Taylor's eye, the locker belonged to Detective Silas Maheny. He opened Silas' locker and stole shoes, a shirt, and pants from the assistant detective. The clothes almost fit, and for now that would have to do.

Taylor was glad that the shoes matched, though the pants and shirt were about a size too small each. The shoes were his now. He decided. Taylor fished through the shirt pockets and found two medium, individually wrapped cigars. He sat down and unwrapped one, enjoying the way Silas' clothes barely fit him, and the smell of his cigar. Taylor found a matchbook in another pocket and lit the cigar. Silas was a dick, but he had good taste in cigars, and Taylor chose to enjoy it until he could leave without killing someone.

]]Chapter 12[[

Taylor strode down the sidewalk with an unnerving glare. He had his temper in check, but that didn't mean he was fine. Whatever was in his eyes, and even he couldn't say without looking in the mirror, was enough to make pedestrians steer clear of his path. A few had made eye contact, briefly, but no one was willing to actually stare at him. He walked slowly, keeping his anger clear, keeping the fog of rage away. His hair was beginning to dry, but for the first time in his adult life he left with it unchecked after the shower. That was fine for right now. The way Silas' clothes didn't fit both helped and hurt. He liked being able to take this out on Silas by stealing his clothes, but they were also a reminder of what had happened. He was walking slowly because he knew if he let himself get worked up again, the next urge would be to bury himself in a drug induced high. And Taylor enjoyed his drugs, but he didn't want to need them, not for this. He didn't want to glaze over his problems, not with the life he led, he'd become a wasted addict in no time. He neared Jackson St. and found himself climbing a sidewalk towards the International District. Flashing lights caught his eye. He found a Pachinko arcade, which didn't appeal to him in the slightest, but he wasn't exactly thinking straight.

Oh what the hell. Taylor pushed the handprint marred door open to Rikkihiro's Pachinko arcade, three buildings down from the oriental overhang of the once famed International District. Cigarette smoke and archaic blips filled the air as he entered. Pachinko games lined the wall from front to back. A wiry haired granny sat in front of her lucky machine, watching tiny steel balls fall every which way, guiding them with a round knob that aimed their trajectory, as the machine convulsed with lights and sound. Pachinko was an ancient form of gambling that worked a little like old pinball machines. The splash of electric colors and sounds made him feel like he had stepped into another country, and after looking at the people slouched in front of the machines, he knew he didn't want to be here long.

Ten minutes of playing and twelve dollars in and Taylor was getting sick of the place. He kept flashing back to the laughs and snickers at Precinct Four. And the worst part was that they were still laughing. Taylor aimed a stream of steel balls to the left and right of a dragon's mouth but they just wouldn't bounce in. Taylor slapped the machine, pushing against the glass and setting off the tilt alarm.

"Hey!" the owner shouted, stomping out from behind his gift counter. Taylor flashed his detective badge. The owner took a look at it and smiled, offering a timid wave and returning to his seat. He was probably hoping Taylor didn't feel the urge to hit any more of his machines, because there was nothing the owner could do about it. Taylor stepped outside. A bar was open across the street. It was almost happy hour, the sun was a few hours past lunchtime.

Taylor had seen this bar a few times and never went inside. In some way it was unappealing. Drab grey colors, a nondescript door, retro neon lights. Whatever his natural tendencies were he just never found himself here. First time for everything.

When he opened the door it wasn't too bad inside. A simple setup of a dark wood grain bar, seven chrome bar stools, and a few tables buried in the corner. For once, simple worked for Taylor. The urge to hit people had faded a bit. Now he could agree to a simple drink. It didn't mean he would descend to the depths of alcoholism. He was calm enough for a regular drink, like a normal guy after a hard day at work. He sat down and played with a napkin while the bartender finished setting his clean cups out. This was a bad day. He was surprised how quickly he was brought back to the old feelings, he thought he had forever left his childhood.

One stupid little prank and the emotions had come right back. Taylor wished he wasn't that vulnerable. He had assumed he wasn't, that he had grown up and could never be hurt again, but today he was taught otherwise.

The bartender approached, a thick gentleman with tufts of grey sprouting past his ears. He smiled like a naughty leprechaun who found the gold long ago. Taylor didn't know if he liked or feared the man. He never saw such a devious smile on so gentle a face. "What can I get ya?" his leprechaun face said.

"Pike's whiskey, leave the bottle," Taylor answered. He shifted in his seat.

Seven shots later and the man was Taylor's new best friend. The bar had filled now. Taylor downed another shot, small glasses lined the bar.

"I'm tellin' ya Joey," as Taylor had began calling him, "…it's more than just a badge. It's a respons… a bili… it's important," he slurred.

The bartender laughed as Taylor slung his arm around him, shouting in his ear. "I'm not Joey, dear lad!" But no matter how many times the bartender corrected him, Taylor kept calling him Joey, which incrementally increased the price of Taylor's drinks.

"What!?" Taylor said, his eyelids half shut. The bartender walked away to another customer. Taylor turned in his seat, tuning in to a conversation he heard on the far side of the bar. Taylor had sat in this chair for hours, watching as bodies filled empty seats. The conversation was about the ban on personal vehicles, griping over lack of freedom and a remembrance of better days. What better days? Taylor's chest tightened. Stupid people pissed him off.

Taylor reached into his pockets, wondering what was in them. This wasn't his suit, it was Silas'. He dug through pockets with clumsy fingers, and smiled. *Silas' badge*. He had been flashing someone elses' badge all night. He also found some cash, a smooth rock, a memory chip,

two breath mints, and a gold watch. Taylor turned to the
man next to him, his back was to Taylor, and slipped the
detective badge into the unsuspecting man's jacket pocket
with a private smirk. Let Silas report it missing. Ha! He
just left Silas' badge in a strange man's jacket. This night
was getting better.

"… damn city cops don't know shit, bunch of bribe
hungry pricks," the man on the far side of the bar said loud
enough to be heard. Taylor stood from his seat.

"What'd you say?" Taylor said. The man was
stocky and early thirties, he looked like he worked
construction, and he hadn't decided what he thought about
Taylor yet.

"Just having a personal conversation, friend, nothing
to do with you," the man said. Two more construction
worker heads turned at Taylor. The one on the left was
covered in white plaster dust and sat considerably shorter
than the other two. All had chiseled forearms from a
lifetime of labor. Damn construction workers, didn't
appreciate the fine work city cops did for them.

"I dun' think you know shit," Taylor said,
accidentally leaning into the shorter man's chair. Taylor
stopped himself but spilled a foamy slosh down the man's
shirt. Barstools peeled back as the three men stood, trunk
arms cocked at their sides.

"Easy, friends!" the bartender shouted. The first
man Taylor had spoken to raised his hands in a calming
gesture. "Just take it easy, pal, go back to your business."

Taylor leaned, the alcohol in him running smooth.
"Joey is my bud, so yer lucky I won't trash his bar. Let's
take dis' ou'side," Taylor slurred. The man he already
spilled beer on stood up to avoid another slosh.

"Look bud," the first man said. "We don't need to
have a problem here, just go back to your drink," but Taylor
cut him off.

"You afraid? Yer mom raised sissies?" Taylor snarled.

The shorter man had heard enough. "You know what? That's it. It's time you learned a lesson," he said, cocking his chair aside. "You need to learn some manners, and I'll teach them to you," he added motioning Taylor outside. Taylor followed the man out through the kitchen and back door. The other two followed behind him. He wasn't planning on kicking everyone's ass, just whup one of them and teach 'em a lesson. A little taste of who they were disrespecting.

Taylor didn't expect it to be so dark when they stepped into the alleyway behind the bar. The only light was from a lamp perched over the back door in the alley.

"You punks' talking to a detect—," Taylor began full of swagger before the man in front of him dropped a lunchbox fist on his chin. Taylor was face down on the wet concrete before he realized he was hit.

"What'd you say about our mommas?!" the taller man said as he kicked Taylor in the ribs. The third man gave another kick in the ribs and then one across the head, cutting Taylor's cheek with his steel toe.

"Hey, that's enough, he's out," the first man jumped in. The three men had barely touched him, all things considered. The tall man looked to kick him again for good measure. His buddy stopped him, resting a hand on his shoulder.

"Forget it, he's done. He's just a drunk," he said, calming his buddy.

"He needs to learn his lesson," the taller one spat. But he let his shoulders relax, tossed his head aside. They looked at Taylor unconscious and snoozing in the alley. "You think he's alright?"

"He's fine, won't feel a thing til' morning," the shorter one laughed.

"Come on, give me a hand. I don't need him getting robbed and killed, I don't want his dead ass on my conscious tomorrow," the first man joked as they reached down to bring Taylor back inside and let him wake up.

A fifth figure stepped out from behind a shadow, no one saw him until that moment.

"Not so fast," the stranger in the alleyway said. He approached them, tall and athletically thick, but otherwise unassuming. He appeared to be finishing a conversation on his telecom. He looked up at them with a look of control as the call ended. "You've just damaged Sethren Company property," the stranger said.

"Just teaching this guy a lesson," the tall construction worker said. His friends took a tentative step away from Taylor's sleeping body when the name Sethren Company was used.

"We don't mean any disrespect to Sethren Company, sir," the one covered in white dust said.

"Gentlemen, it's far too late for that," the stranger declared, his voice dangerously calm. The three exchanged glances.

All at once the stranger lunged, sliding over Taylor's body and thrusting his hand out. A blade flashed at the tallest of the three. Then the stranger spun. The tall one convulsed as the shorter one clutched at his throat. The last man gaped in horror as his friends collapsed. He tried to run away while the stranger's back was to him, but the stranger bounded on him. His arm snaked around the neck and squeezed until he felt it snap.

A van approached, unmarked. The stranger walked over to Taylor and pulled Taylor's body gently out of the way. The van stopped and its doors opened. A crew of three climbed out and tossed the three dead men in the back of the van and shut the door.

As the stranger waited for the cleaners he turned his head to the side, avoiding the booze smell emanating from Taylor. *Degenerates*. He activated his telecom device.

"It's done sir. Taylor is fine. He'll wake up in his office. No sir, he was completely unconscious. His face was cut. His rib has a hairline crack. Nothing serious sir, he'll be fine. Thank you sir," the stranger said. Jack's concern for Taylor was a mystery to the stranger, but it wasn't his place to judge. He only needed to know what his orders were. As long as Taylor doesn't get himself killed, his mission is a success.

]]Chapter 13[[

"Taylor? Taylor! Wake up!"

Taylor's head popped up off his desk, his eyes darted to the wall clock.

"Taylor!!"

Vina stood in front of him. Taylor scrubbed crust from his eyes with both hands, wondering why his ribs hurt. He had never slept that hard, and that was saying something.

"What are you doing here?" he said forcing one eyelid ajar to see.

"You called."

"I called?" The desk phone lay toppled over on the table, a bottle of painkiller empty in his left hand. He pushed it off the desk and clumsily straightened up all the loose files and folders. He moved to stand until his rib cried out, though it throbbed a bit less than his jaw. Together they hurt far less than his head. He felt like he had his ass kicked.

"What's the big emergency, Taylor?"

Did I call her? Taylor was too disoriented to remember. He was at the Pachinko arcade, he went to a bar, all of it fogged over like a dream and nothing like a memory. He made it to the precinct…that much was clear.

"Taylor, your face," she said with a look that demanded an explanation.

Taylor touched his cheek to feel the blood crusted on his face. The swirling events of yesterday pooled down into his stomach, he snatched the waste bin and dry heaved.

"Is this just another hangover?" Vina grew impatient.

"Happy Anniversary," Taylor said. He didn't know. He was just as confused as her. "Vina…" he struggled to say, stretching the sleep away.

"Hop in the shower. You stink. I'll come back

later." Vin was always someone who couldn't say no. She *always* helped. Maybe that's why she tried to stay with Taylor as long as she did, until she just couldn't take it anymore. Taylor wretched again into the waste bin and didn't realize she had left until minutes later when he looked up. He really felt sore; he must have had his ass kicked last night. A little while later a trepid knock came.

"Yeah…?"

"Detective?" A face peeked out from behind the door. *An officer*? It shouldn't be a surprise, he worked in a police station, but it did surprise him. No one ever visited him. Plus they pulled a prank on him yesterday.

"What can I do for you Sgt….?"

"Sgt Briggs," he said stepping the rest of the way in. "No offense, Detective, I heard you were back. We all kind of thought that…well after you disappeared…," Sgt Briggs had trouble saying it.

"That I was dead?"

"More or less sir. You know, a lot of us were against that prank, sir. Me and a buddy took care of the guy that did it, so to speak, sir,"

"Oh," Taylor said. He fell into silence, unsure of what to say. This was a mildly empathic gesture, he was completely surprised by it. "Well, I'm not dead, sorry."

Sgt Briggs nodded, and slowly excused himself. He looked about to say something else, but changed his mind. Taylor rose from his chair, body stiff, and leaned against the wall for support all the way to Catheri's office. Catheri walked in the door, fresh and ready to start her day. She looked at his face and the blood down his neck, questions forming at the edge of her lips.

"I'll be in the shower if Vin returns. Schedule me a medic."

"This makes two days in a row that you came to work before me. I don't know if I'm more worried about that, or by the bruises on your face," Catheri said. Her words were un-invested, but Taylor saw how worried she was. He ignored her and limped past her. It took a little longer than normal to get down the hallway, he was still wearing the soiled, torn, and barely fitting clothes he *borrowed* from Detective Silas Maheny. He held his side as he hobbled past the officers who only yesterday jeered and made bets. Today they collaborated in blank stares.

"Somebody still owes me a shirt," Taylor growled. At the locker room he undressed, hanging the rags back in Maheny's locker. The pockets were empty, he remembered emptying them on the bar counter last night, and he remembered giving away Silas' detective badge. That made him laugh, and then cry as he forgot his rib was broken. His naked body hobbled into the shower.

Taylor closed his eyes, the warm water rinsed away more than blood and sweat. A shower had never felt so good. Taylor chuckled. He got out and dried himself slowly, taking care with his rib and jaw. In the mirror he inspected the gash on his face. It stretched a few inches from the top of his smile. He would have to do something about that.

Taylor opened his locker to find that Catheri had replaced his stained shirts with fresh ones and pressed slacks. It had to be her, she was the only person in the department who would do as much. Everyone else hated him. Catheri looked up to greet him when he returned. A paper note lay folded on her table with Taylor's name on it.

"Who delivered this?"

"I don't know, it arrived last night. What happened to you?" Catheri finally asked.

"It was just there?"

"Yes," she answered, waiting for Taylor to answer her in turn.

Instead he paced the room with the note in hand. He knew he could trust Catheri. He unfolded the note and read the inside. It was a list of salvage records, scrap metals, and unclaimed materials all documented from a salvage crew dated thirty years ago. Taylor exhaled, long and slow, and chuckled at the end. False alarm. For a minute he thought it was going to be something important, though beyond that he didn't know what he was expecting. This was a useless list, probably from the same person who hacked his Spec7, and Taylor already had enough of that game. Taylor tossed the note but missed the trash.

"Where's the backup telecom? My phone went…missing," Taylor said. He didn't need to divulge the whole story, especially since he didn't know it.

Catheri slid open a desk drawer and retrieved a bulky department issued portable com. She stood to hand it to him and suddenly wrapped her arms around him, kissing him on the lips. Taylor sort of kissed her back. "I'm late, I have to go," he said taking the phone from her.

Catheri looked down at the ground, shaking off her embarrassment. "Commander Keeb is looking for you," she said just before he left, but he ignored that. He especially ignored that. He had already spent too long in Precinct Four over the last few days.

Taylor walked carefully and deliberately, his rib wouldn't let him get away with more than that. He used the wall for support, discretely, he didn't need the attention of someone asking if he was okay. He approached the holding cells on his right, which he never looked in because he was usually in a hurry, but due to his slow pace he had a second to gaze inside and see an old friend of his. Taylor stopped. Ayne was in a chair, hands cuffed behind her, oval eyes staring blankly at the wall. Her makeup was smudged, which gave her an exotic look. Confidence, that's what Ayne had, and that's why Taylor couldn't forget her. She was so different now. Taylor took her in, head to toe, with every lace and skirt and strap in between. Some would think she dressed like a prostitute, but Ayne never went that route, at least not that he knew of. Everyone who sat in that chair had a look about them, the look told you everything. If they looked afraid, they were guilty, or they knew something. If they didn't look afraid, they were usually guilty too, but were too seasoned to care. Ayne looked like she didn't care and never had, and the sooner someone got her out of here, prison or otherwise, the less pissed she would be.

"What's with her?" Taylor asked the officer on duty. The officer seemed shocked that Taylor had spoken to him. Officer... Taylor didn't know his name.

"Her? POV infraction, no license, also almost ran over a cop."

"You don't say," Taylor laughed. The officer went back to what he was doing before Taylor had interrupted him. That was worth a year in prison, more for a girl with Ayne's record. When nobody was looking, Taylor unlocked Ayne's holding cell with his detective badge and walked in.

"Ayne, hello again."

Her face dropped when Taylor walked in. He must have left an impression on her, unintentionally of course. Taylor sat down at the desk across from her, a computer uplink came out of the desktop. He accessed the internal network, typing into the desk's keyboard. He looked up at her, she glared back with snake-like contempt. He accessed Ayne's file and cancelled her interrogation, next he adjusted the length of her detainment, erasing the records of her recent infraction. Now she would be released within an hour. But she didn't know that yet.

"There are other ways to visit me," Taylor smiled.

"The *Butchers* protect me," she said suddenly.

"And?" Ayne was actually trying to protect herself by naming a street gang. She must be truly scared, but damn, she did not look it.

"How did you get in with them?" Taylor asked. She blinked, and after a puzzling silence she finally answered.

"Family."

"Orphan's don't have families," Taylor laughed.

She looked at him in a way that meant Taylor had just made a mistake.

"Family is more than blood," she answered, almost offended. Suddenly she cocked her head at Taylor. There was a new look in her. "You don't have one, do you?"

"A street gang? No," Taylor laughed.

"A family," she said. Taylor's response, or lack of response, told Ayne she was dead on. Now it was Ayne that was smiling. "Oohhh poor baby, you have mommy issues, don't you. I'm starting to get you now," she said. Taylor pressed a couple keys on the keyboard and slammed it shut.

"Well, no more joyrides, and we're even. Do we have a deal?" Taylor said. She didn't know what he meant, but she would in about an hour. He left the room, locking the computer before he left, and refusing to look at Ayne again. He could be fired for what he just did, but he didn't think twice about it. At the moment he was only thinking about himself, and the way Ayne had shut him down, effortlessly. What just happened? Taylor didn't have issues with being an orphan. He didn't have issues about anything.

Taylor finally went outside, kicking himself. He shouldn't have stopped by those holding cells, he should just leave Ayne alone and jerk off to her in peace. Not that it was a sexual thing with her, actually he didn't know what it was with her. He didn't understand why he thought of her, why he followed her, bullied her. Taylor squinted from the morning sun. A small gust of wind carried the smell of seaweed through the city. Aside from the humidity it was shaping up to be nice and sunny. He saw Vina coming up the sidewalk. She looked… weightless.

"Taylor, when I said I wanted to be there for you, I meant something a little different," Vina said. "Why did you call me last night?"

Taylor was silent, he didn't know why he called her. He passed reply after reply through his head. He wanted to say something, but he didn't know what. He had so many emotions lately, it wasn't like him. He closed his mouth, swallowed the apologies he was about to make, the things he was about to say. "Must have misdialed," Taylor said.

Vina rolled her eyes and exhaled. "This is serious," she said in a firm voice. Her face said it all. "Fine. Sure. Good bye, Taylor," she said. Taylor watched Vina disappear down the street. It hurt to see her go, but she needed to go. She couldn't waste herself on Taylor anymore. Taylor started walking. No point making the medic wait.

"You know we can't make any more of these?" the medic sighed, pointing to the nanobot repair vials. Taylor had to threaten him before the medic admitted even having them. They were worth a small fortune on the black market.

"Just shut up and do it, doc." Taylor wasn't about to go away empty handed. The doctor had failed to dissuade Taylor, who once again leveraged the weight of his detective badge. The good medic felt these precious nanobots were reserved for High Generals, Chancellors, Heads of State, etc. The medic considered the wavering needle full of nanobot solution before cramming it into Taylor's shoulder. Taylor smiled at the pinch. This was more like himself. Getting his way, not caring what people thought. The injection warmed and vibrated like an old battery.

"My rib still hurts," Taylor mocked, scratching at the back of his head.

"It takes time," the medic snapped. Taylor was already grabbing his jacket. He hated the smell of sterile surfaces. He made sure to leave the door open as he left.

It took a few hours but eventually he could walk without a limp and twist at the waist a bit. Most importantly his face tingled as little bots stimulated cell regeneration.

That was good, he didn't need a scar ruining his winning smile. The rest was up to good old fashioned healing, nanobots had a short cell life and the little things ended up as kidney fodder. The body took over after their little jump start.

That afternoon he returned to the precinct. Ayne had been released due to an administrative error. Funny how things worked out. Commander Keeb still hadn't called, that almost worried Taylor. Yesterday still didn't seem real, he'd have called it a dream if not for the pain. He should be dead but today it was like nothing ever happened. If there was a moral here he'd probably forget it by dinner. He knew one thing; a killer was still loose in this city, and Taylor was the only one who would stop him. He didn't know his next step, but he knew his best ideas came to him while cruising.

So Taylor rode the lightrail transits to nowhere specific. He stopped and worked a vending machine to grab puffed cheese snacks and then roamed some more. The transits swelled with commuters, an unfortunate blend of colognes and hair gels crowded the seats next to him. He didn't know where to go, except that he didn't want to be in the office. He didn't really have a home now that Vina had kicked him out. Taylor was surprised at how he felt about that, he didn't care once, not until she did it. Now he almost missed her.

A fatherly man wearing glasses stared at Taylor. Taylor noticed him three stops ago, he never saw the man before but that didn't keep the man from staring. Taylor finally stared back, wondering what was up. The man wore a gold wristwatch, nothing electronic, just elegant and classic. Whatever else this man was, he was interested in Taylor. When the lightrail stopped and the man stepped off Taylor followed. Time to see where this went.

Lower Fifth Avenue. Its cultural past was now a bastard present. The former center of theatre and art was now infested with a brand of lawlessness that even cops steered clear of. The stranger on the lightrail did not belong here. Taylor walked up the aged concrete steps from the underground station, which had been painted over not once but countless times by seemingly anyone with a paintbrush. Light bounced off the glass windows of the theater, bringing a little life to the tired colors of this once famous block. He had never seen it in the daytime, it looked undead, if a building could. Taylor didn't need to try to find the man from the lightrail. He was waiting for Taylor next to the old Fifth Ave Theatre.

Taylor looked around, half convinced this was an elaborate trap. Not that he was special enough for such an elaborate plan. He just didn't understand where this was coming from, and he half wanted to disappear without finding out. He knew it was best to trust his instincts, but his curiosity usually won in the end. "Do we know each other?" Taylor asked walking up to the man. The man hid his hands in his pockets. Taylor hated not seeing the hands, too many bad surprises could pop out. Taylor realized he left his blaster at the precinct. He stood a little closer than he otherwise would, just in case this stranger had something stupid in mind.

"Did you get my note?"

"What note?" Taylor replied. The stranger gave a look that said 'why am I not surprised'. Taylor was almost offended, the man couldn't possibly know anything about him. But then he remembered, the mysterious note that Catheri gave him earlier. Taylor opened his mouth but didn't speak. Of all the imaginary faces his mystery man had, old man river here wasn't on the list. If he was following *this* guy's clues, he had to rethink his career as a detective.

"Yeah, your garbage list. Can't say it helped," Taylor said looking around. Was this a setup? Or just a waste of time.

"The information on that note wasn't something for office clerks and wandering eyes. You were supposed to look a bit deeper. You are a detective, right?"

"Alledgedly. Who the hell are you?"

"I'm a scientist, of the old arts by your definition. I'm Jack Sethren's golden goose."

Taylor shut his mouth the moment he realized it was gaping. Of the old arts? Those guys were a myth, extinct, long gone. The scientists of today knew almost nothing of the old techs. The technology crisis was a result of such lost knowledge. If this man was what he said he was, and Taylor thought he might be, he was worth Jack Sethren's entire fortune. He could change the world. And Taylor stood with him in a place like Old Fifth Ave, where chemically mummified corpses did three animatronic shows a day.

"How does space debris relate to our murders?"

"Getting better, detective. Do you remember the Purge of Knowledge, the great loss of information during the war? Let me tell you about Jack Sethren. He gained power with the United Modern Americans by being ruthless. He hunted exiles and butchered them. You know about the genocides? He embraced the concept. But one episode holds specific importance to you and me, the Space Station Hephaestus. That's where the last of the old scientists hid in an attempt to preserve knowledge, to protect the technologies our species had developed before they were lost to those dark times. Jack… found me there. His troops did what they came to do. I survived."

"You're boring the shit out of me."

The scientist looked down, frustrated by Taylor, and his jacket opened ever so briefly. There was something under his jacket, Taylor knew it. "You'll catch on. Ten years ago an old *project* of mine returned to me, from Hephaestus. That's where your killer comes in. He's not human, but he thinks he is. Or he once was, depending on how you look at it. I made him either way, but someone else finished him."

The story suddenly mattered. "What?" Taylor shook his head. "Your robot is the killer?"

"Can't you appreciate complexity? Or must you dumb it down to something in a single sentence so your mind can understand it."

"I dumb it down."

"I see." The man's face softened. "My time is up, my sins must be atoned for. I've come to ponder on many things, Taylor. Things like redemption. I'm a scientist of the old ways, and yet my knowledge can't be shared. Sethren Company uses what I know for power, as if power was what mattered. Technology should be used to help people, not control them. One of these days I'll have to tell you about it. You deserve that much."

"What about Jack Sethren? You said the robot was the killer," Taylor asked. The scientist smiled a sad smile. He chose to ignore Taylor's question.

"I should have died with my brethren. I thought I was lucky, once." The scientist smiled in a sad way, and then produced a blaster from inside his jacket. Taylor grabbed at his wrist but he was stronger than anticipated. A shot fired, blood splattered on the wall.

"He just shot that guy!" a witness pointed at Taylor. Taylor didn't shoot anyone, but from every angle it looked that way. Taylor ducked into the theater and wound his way down the seats to the stage entrance, seeking a new exit. He tried wiping his face clean but it did little more than smear the red blood. Taylor shook his hands clean. The theater had five spectators bathed in low light, the stage aimed to please those with a fetish for the macabre. He pushed open a door leading off stage where actors dressed. He saw a mirror, and the scientist's blood all over his face. He poured water from a sink, blood turned the porcelain bowl red.

Fifth Ave, where no one would be surprised, where a rich man would be killed for his watch, seven days a week.

||Chapter 14||

     The beginning of John's vengeance, before it had a face, before it had life, started in the desolation of outer space, in freezing temperatures, waiting for death or madness. Drifting in space, the cold proved to be the greatest challenge. Sanity had already fled him. John's lamp was just a salvaged monitor screen, and with its soft light he had found all sorts of things inside the cargo lock. The container that was his home, his prison, his tomb. Most of the items here were his life's accomplishments. His work, the furthering of science and technology on the space station, had led to many exotic creations. It wasn't all his, there were other scientists working here, but he had a hand in most of it. It was a tragedy all its own, the greatest achievements in history, lost to the carnages of war. How long would it take humanity to regain what it lost here?

     Precious cargo perched quietly along the metal wall, all magnetically sealed to the floor to keep from floating during transport. Out of necessity, out of desperation to find meaning in his death, John ripped one open, spilling its contents into the weightless air. At first he sought something that could end his penance. But the time spent examining the various devices, tools, cables, and electronic components became a relief from the cold. And his demons.

     He examined each item as a child would, as if seeing them for the first time. Many items he really was seeing for the first time. It kept his mind away from the cold, giving him a purpose, a meaning, to search for something. Feverishly John ripped open the next crate, its guts floating out in front of him. Hours went by as he poured over the gadgets. A telescope. A neutron agitator shaped like a melon. A holographic DNA study aid with touch interactivity for students. A music box. A tube for studying proton density. Crate after crate revealed its cargo to him, soon he couldn't cross the room without bumping across some piece of cutting edge technology floating in his path.

Crystals were forming around his mouth and nose, he took a few breaths before readying to continue. The constant dimness affected his sense of time. He would not fall asleep to an audience of haphazard objects casting moving shadows, the panic of waking would be too much. Better not to let his body rest. He hoisted a pipe and ripped open another large, upright case.

From within the blackness of the storage container two blue metallic eyes opened, illuminating the subtle contours of a human face behind them. John screamed and flailed backwards, knocking into floating heaps of junk. He sank into the mess of boxes and packaging materials behind him.

"NO!! HELP!!" he screamed. False images flooded his fragile mind, visions he knew couldn't be real. It took minutes for his panic to fade, and when he looked in the crate again, he saw the eyes were still there. They were real. This was the beginning of his vengeance. Here, the androids would become John's dying wish, to punish those who were responsible, however long it took. John hadn't realized it yet, but his revenge was still alive.

Vina tucked her robe around her before answering the door, whoever was knocking at this horrible hour would not go away. It was three in the morning. Vina already suspected she would see Taylor in the peephole to the hallway outside. She didn't take joy in being right.

"Taylor? It's three in the morning!"

This wasn't Taylor's house anymore, Vina even

installed new keys. Come to think of it she didn't know where Taylor was living.

"He shot himself... I was talking to him and he shot himself…"

"What? Keep your voice down, who shot himself?" Vina urged.

"He thinks he left me some clue, but there's nothing! It's just a stupid piece of paper!"

"Please keep your voice down," she shushed him again. Taylor looked past her.

"You alone?" Taylor asked.

"Damn you, Taylor, I can't do this." She walked back inside, tightening her robe. Taylor followed. "Taylor, it's three in the morning."

"Right… ah, breakfast? I'll cook," he said.

"You can't just show up here."

Taylor slouched in the doorway to the other room. He knew that, but he didn't have anywhere else to go. His head rested wearily against the wall. "Vin…"

"Taylor it's three in the morning. Why are you here?"

"He shot himself."

"Who?"

"I don't know what to do, Vin."

"Taylor…I *can't* help you…"

Taylor knocked his head softly against the wall. She was right, he had done enough to her already. He gave a weak smile and left for the door.

"Taylor, wait..." Vin said.

He did not stop, but he did close the door softly. Vina didn't need his problems. She had her own problems. He couldn't ask her for anything. He could deal with this on his own. He didn't know the guy, and those dumb clues weren't helping Taylor in any way. Taylor wondered where he was going as he boarded, rode, and exited the lightrail. He found himself standing on Catheri's street. No. She didn't need his problems either.

        The precinct was his only home now, and he went
there instead. He had not slept since waking at his desk that
morning, and from the night earlier he still owed himself a
week in the spa. That felt like a lifetime ago. Taylor
thought about his old friend, Ms. Payer.

        He rarely thought about Ms. Payer. He tried never
to think of her. Ms. Payer was the one person who had been
kind to him, practically throughout his entire life. She used
to be his school teacher, but she practically became his
mother. She saw something in him that no one else did, and
she was kind to him. She was the only one who had made
him a birthday cake, when she realized no one else ever had.
Taylor could still smell the burnt smoke coming out of the
oven.

        A late duty officer knocked on the door as Taylor
stood staring at the wall, almost dozing away to sleep.
"Detective?" he asked. He was a junior officer.

        "Yeah," Taylor said.

        "I just wanted to say, you know, some of the guy's
are behind you. We want you to find this guy," he said. He
may as well have swiped Taylor's feet out from under him.

        Was I just thanked for something? he wondered. He
wasn't sure if that had ever happened before.

        "Not sure what you mean, officer," Taylor said.

        "I respect Keeb and all, sir, but cops aren't stupid.
Keeb's covering something up, and Silas is helping him. It's
nice to see someone stand up to him, that's all," he said.

        Taylor thought about what this officer said for a
moment. They thought Taylor was standing up to Keeb?
Actually, Taylor was just being a bad cop. But somehow, in
light of how Commander Keeb was viewed, that made
Taylor look defiant. Perhaps noble? Taylor could honestly
say he wasn't expecting a rallying of morale to be the result
of his many insubordinations. "Those are dangerous
opinions, better keep them to yourself if you know what I

mean," Taylor warned. The officer didn't take offense, that was simply good advice when it came to talking about Commander Keeb. Taylor was at a momentary loss for words. Precinct Four was becoming divided between Commander Keeb's loyal men, and the misguided others who thought of Taylor as their shining knight. As flattering as it was, the last thing Taylor needed was a support team. He didn't want people to have to live up to. Taylor climbed into the chair at his desk and pondered this until sleep finally took him.

He awoke, starving for breakfast. He looked at the time, it was six in the morning, which was about two hours of sleep, that was it. *Nuts.*

Taylor stood, scratching his head to wake up. *Food.* The food at the precinct wasn't fit for prisoners, and nothing within a city mile was open. So as much as he regretted it, he boarded the lightrail. At six in the morning he was almost alone on New Seattle City's great transportation achievement. A grizzled man was snoring on the floor between seats, there were three teenagers who had never seen daylight, and a man who looked uncomfortable in his own skin. The man had either just killed someone or cheated on his wife for the first time.

No one paid Taylor any mind. He was alone with those cryptic last words, a puzzle to keep Taylor awake. Did the scientist make some kind of confession? What did he confess? And those stupid clues? Taylor spent hours reading that note, there wasn't anything there!

All of this had something to do with Jack Sethren, the dead scientist, and his robot project. In a way Taylor knew much, but nothing he could go on. Who was the next kill? Taylor rubbed his temples. He hated thinking this much. Just do the job.

The lightrail hushed to a stop. A person boarded and sat behind Taylor as he closed his eyes to catch a moment of rest. He could sleep right here, just like the bum.

"Early bird still catches the worm, eh?" Taylor asked

the person behind him. There was a long silence.

How do you mean?" a little girl's voice replied.
She sounded no more than ten, which surprised Taylor. He
didn't get a look at her when she boarded, but he would have
noticed a little kid. And it was six in the morning. Not that
he was an expert, but who let their daughter out this early?

"I'm just talking about life," Taylor replied. Taylor
closed his eyes, and remembered why he kept to himself.
Lack of sleep must be making him loopy. "Do your parents
know you are out this late?" he joked. Was he so out of
touch when it came to kids these days?

"My daddy sent me. He sends me to find stuff for
him," she said.

"What do you find?" Taylor asked. Small hairs on
the back of his neck stirred.

"I find the fuckers he is looking for," she said.

What? Taylor's senses suddenly stood on end.
What did that girl just say?

The train stopped, she stepped off the cabin and
Taylor took a real look at her. The girl was tall, much too
tall for a ten year old, and wearing a trench coat with the
hood pulled up. There was something else. As the train
gave a customary pause before closing the doors, Taylor saw
her face, smooth and pale, almost artificial. Was her skin
modified? She looked like a mannequin. Now he had seen
it all. *Freaks*. He tapped his foot. She looked as if someone
manufactured her.

"Wait!"

]]Chapter 15[[

Taylor jumped off of his seat and barely exited the lightrail as the doors closed shut. The air stirred as the transports lifted and sped away behind him. Early morning feet began pouring down the steps, but Taylor's eyes were on the girl in the trench coat, her and Taylor being the only sets of eyes facing away from the lightrails. She was standing still, long, artificial black hair oblivious to the jets of air formed by the transports. Taylor suspected she was aware of his presence. She turned and looked Taylor in the eye, and her face sent a chill down his spine. Coincidentally, Taylor remembered his blaster was still back at the office. She turned to run.

"HEY!"

Taylor charged, and she ran. She more than ran, she practically catapulted up the steps to the street level. Taylor couldn't match her speed, no chance in hell. He ran up the stairs and glimpsed her plow someone over before turning down an alleyway. How was he going to catch her? Judging by how the person she knocked over was struggling to get up, she was strong. Very strong. He didn't know what his plan of attack was, exactly, except that it would probably be easier to catch her now than to try and find her again. He wouldn't get this lucky twice. "Get back here!"

Taylor ran across the street, shielding the first rays of sun from his eyes, and finally rounded the entrance to the alleyway. He found it was a dead end, and Taylor saw that she was huddled in the corner, frightened. Taylor was surprised to see her there, for a few reasons. The first was that she was obviously much faster than he was. The second was that Taylor was expecting a male robot, if gender mattered. The scientist had referred to it as a *he,* just before committing suicide on Fifth Ave. But Taylor wasn't going to get hung up on that detail. He really had to take a second look at it, if he didn't know better it really was a person.

"Don't move, you're under arrest," he said while carefully approaching, wondering how he might enforce that. She actually looked scared, at least until Taylor got closer. Suddenly she stood and faced the wall, no longer looking like a frightened child. In the next instant, she plowed *through* the wall, tearing a hole through it.

Lights in the alleyway flickered and sparks showered where she tore through the wall, cutting cables, wires, and bricks alike. Taylor dove through the fresh hole in the wall and ran through the new back entrance of a deli kitchen. Two prep cooks huddled around a small table and looked up as if the angel of death had come.

An explosion of glass came from the next room, Taylor followed the sounds of destruction. It was still dark in the customer seating area, he could only see mere outlines of tables and chairs. He cut to the other side of the room and darted through the exit it had made in the lobby window, tripping on his way outside. After scrambling to his feet he looked up to see her running. Taylor would never catch up to her.

An overhang perched within leaping distance, Taylor jumped and climbed and scrambled himself onto the roof of a pawn shop. He was tired of chasing her through whatever path she could create. Squat rooftops stretched this city block, and he had a better view of her from up here. Taylor ran to the far side of the roof. He jumped across, sprinting to keep her in sight.

She disappeared down the steps to another lightrail station. Taylor approached a split in the rooftops, a narrow alleyway waited meters below. He leapt across, racing to find her again, dodging around smoke coming out of a ventilation drain. She wasn't in view anymore, and Taylor felt his only lead slipping away. He had to find a way to get down now, a garbage bin was on his left, but he dreaded what unknown objects may break his fall. Instead Taylor swung a leg over the rooftop ledge and carefully found the drain pipe. He was hoping it would hold his wait, until his foot slipped and he fell.

"Aghh!" He landed hard, his ankle shot pain up and down his leg. He made himself upright and hobbled towards the entry and down the steps to the transit. He couldn't let her disappear. The air stirred with the electric hum of an oncoming lightrail, barely audible amid the chatter of morning commuters. The stations were filling to the brim. Pedestrian rush hour had started.

Taylor hobbled frantically, gripping the handrail and taking each step one by one down. His ankle wasn't ready to have weight on it yet, but he knew it wasn't broken, mostly because nothing had popped. When he made it to the bottom it took him several looks to spot her among the commuters. She would have blended in if he didn't already know her coat, she had covered her hair with the hood. Suddenly she turned and looked over her shoulder, Taylor kept hidden behind the man in front of him as best he could. She faced back to the front. The train arrived, doors opened, passengers herded onboard, and the doors closed. Taylor watched her stand still the whole time, she never boarded. He was glad, he needed a moment to catch his breath. After a moment it was just Taylor, the robot, and a homeless fellow asleep by the wall.

"Okay, now how am I going to do this," Taylor wondered to himself.

The lightrail picked up speed, and as it did, as Taylor was wondering how he was going to arrest her, she ran forward and leapt *into* the plexi-wall of the cabin, demolishing her way inside it. A wave of shrieks erupted from a dozen terrified commuters. Taylor sprinted after her, there was no plan, only desperation. The last cabin on the lightrail was in view and Taylor bolted forward, leaping for it before it disappeared after the rest of the train. He landed on a small platform at the very end, firmly grabbing a maintenance handle and slamming into the back cabin from the momentum. A moment's hesitation and he would have missed it completely. The train picked up speed at a pitiless rate, Taylor held on for all he was worth. He never realized how fast these things moved until he found himself dangling on the outside of one.

Taylor pulled himself up as it reached traveling speed, the cries still came from the demolished cabin, blending with the sounds of rushing wind. He unpinned the side of his face from the bulkhead and tried to spot her through the window chain of the cabins. The panic she had created kept him from seeing any farther than the first few seats however, too many heads were in the way, too many people scared and crushing each other in fear. Thankfully he felt the lightrail slowing, the next stop was coming. And it was a good thing, his grip was feeling very weak.

The train stopped. The sleepy commuters waiting for the train were practically toppled when the doors opened and terrified people came screaming out. Over the cacophony of confused shrieks, Taylor heard a siren blaring in the distance. Someone had alerted the police about a disturbance, which was one word for it. That changed things, he knew he was running out of time and options. Taylor had to find a way to end this or contain it before she disappeared for good. While his fellow officers would be studying what looked like a terrorist attack on the lightrails, his robo-bitch would be disappearing into the crowd. If he had his blaster he might be able to do something about it. He needed to get his hands on one, and fast. Taylor took a long, deep breath and shook his hands out. He thought better when he was loose, and he needed to give himself a rest after clinging to the back of lightrail for dear life. What the hell made him do that?

Still resting on the back of the cabin, Taylor glanced through the chain of inner windows. There wasn't a soul on them, nor was his robot there, which meant she had fled with the crowd. He looked out into the mob of people, scanning for her. There were so many bodies running, so many people confused, and more than a handful who just sat there wondering what the fuss was about. Taylor didn't see her, and maybe that was a good thing. He hadn't been thinking straight. He couldn't stop her. Taylor knew when his butt was kicked, maybe it was best to try again later when he did have a blaster on him. But, after thinking about it for a minute, he knew himself better than that. Taylor cracked his knuckles and stretched his neck. *I'm not finished yet.* Taylor didn't have his blaster, but he *did* have his telecom.

"Catheri. Are you on your way to work yet? I need something…"

Taylor did a small dance up the steps to street level, humming a tune to himself. *This* was the real him, the guy who never listened, not even to himself. Two officers responding to the disturbance at the lightrail hustled past him down the steps. They would have a hard time explaining the damage in the wall. But Taylor wasn't about to write any reports, he was just waiting for Catheri to show up. The android girl had walked up the steps, which meant she thought she had lost him. He was good with that.

The steps led to a stretch of restaurants, hotels, and the best coffee in New Seattle City. Taylor wondered if this was her home or if it was just the first stop she took to try to lose him. He approached a bench on the sidewalk and stood on it, peering across the bobble of heads moving up and down the street. When Taylor saw her, tall and unnatural, sliding among people like a wolf through a herd of sheep, his adrenaline came back. He hopped down and eyed her from a distance, watching as she entered a cafe. Taylor walked to the far side of the street, keeping an eye on the cafe while hiding behind a noodle soup vending machine. It would be best if he didn't spook her again, not yet. He redialed Catheri with unsteady fingers, damn adrenaline shakes. He took a long breath, he could do this.

"Catheri, where are you? I'm near Café Bella. Hurry and I'll buy you a cup," he said. Taylor chewed the bottom of his lip as he ended the call. Here he was, perched one blaster away from solving this entire murder case and getting his life back in order. He would become the hero who stopped a killer robot, which he didn't know of anyone else ever doing, and he would be forever endowed with major clout as a Detective. Even Keeb would be forced to pin a medal on Taylor after swallowing his manhood worth of pride.

Taylor would have a free pass to do what he wanted to, because Keeb wouldn't be able to touch a public hero. The city would name a street in his honor. Parents would name their firstborn children Taylor. And it was all five minutes away from happening. Taylor didn't know how these daydreams came to him so easily, but they did.

The android waited in her seat near the window, alienated from the world around her. No one noticed her, but that wasn't uncommon in a city like this. People kept to themselves, even a man dying in the street would see people walking by. That, and at first glance she looked like someone who was modded, not obviously a robot. Taylor was bouncy, he prayed she didn't get up and leave. This spot was public, and perfect.

Four minutes later Catheri came walking up the street, a shopping bag in her hand. The morning sun was rousing, holding everything in a stiff early grey. Men and jealous women watched Catheri anywhere she went. She always looked stunning. Taylor realized he had never seen her without makeup and perfect hair, not even in the morning.

"A bit early to be hunting, isn't it Detective?" She handed the bag to Taylor who held it unwillingly. This was a *lady's* shopping bag, big and pink.

"This?" he questioned.

"I can't carry a hand-cannon in public, it makes people nervous," Catheri said. She was the only girl who would carry a gun in a shopping bag for him. It made him feel warm inside.

"Really?" Taylor asked and then ripped the bag away. He held a department issue ultra magnum blaster, easily capable of shooting through walls. Catheri had a gift for getting the best gear from the Supply chief. It was as if she had slept with the guy. Taylor considered the blaster and her warning. "Maybe you're right." With a loose stride he crossed the street, a look in his eyes.

Taylor pushed open the door to the café, his badge hanging out over his shirt, the blaster held loosely at his side. There were lots of witnesses to tell the tale of this day. The android turned her head, looking him in the eye. Taylor raised the blaster, cupping it with both hands, and fired a shot so loud it shook the coffee cups. The table shredded into thin air, her face froze in artificial terror as she flew through the window and crashed to the street. Damn, this gun packed a punch! Taylor's forearms tingled from the jolt of the blast. He followed her outside, climbing out the window he just destroyed, careful not to cut himself with a shard of glass. The morning sun made her glow on the concrete, her robotic truth suddenly naked to everyone. She was trying to get up, mechanically unable to, since part of her torso was missing. Now the morning herd of commuters stopped, realizing something was happening. Eyes widened and mouths gasped. Taylor heard their questions, their whispers, their shock. An android? Yes. Take it in while you can, Taylor thought.

Taylor raised the cannon and blasted again, the sound was much easier on his ears this time, being outside and all. Her chest erupted into sparks, pieces of metal and plastic ricocheted from her body, clattering meters away down the street. Her body jolted in a confusion of useless signals. Taylor had never seen an android die before. He had never even seen one, actually. Sparks crackled from loose circuits, her arms and legs convulsed. The wave of gasps swelled from the citizens watching. Taylor meant to take a look around, to let everyone see who had done this, to flash his badge proudly. But he didn't. Or, he couldn't. Instead he watched her die in the street, until she was unmoving, and saw the light in her eyes go completely dark.

Taylor held this moment, trying to taste his victory, before turning to address a very nervous Catheri. The taste was not as sweet as he expected. It was almost bitter.

"Call it in."

]]Chapter 16[[

The faces inside the container John opened had triggered a flashback from Hephaestus. He yanked on the door trying to escape, a useless effort. He spoke to the container, eventually, afraid of what might answer back. Over time John grew less afraid. He grew less cold too, and that was a very wonderful thing even if it meant deep hypothermia.

"It's okay daddy, they won't hurt us," his little girl told him. She rested a hand on his shoulder. John smiled, it was so good to see her.

"Thanks kiddo," John said. "HELLO?" John called.

"Don't yell daddy, save your strength," his little girl urged him.

"What's in there?"

"Don't you remember daddy? The androids they built?" she asked.

"Yes... of course you're right. I forgot, that's all," John told her.

She was right, she was always right. He pulled himself towards them, coaxing himself along as he saw their faces again. He did recognize them. The android on the left was the most complete, she almost looked like a person. The male was a step behind cosmetically, larger and more obvious. Both were operational, or at least the manifest said so when John checked.

John remembered this project. These androids were designed before the genocides and were set aside until their future could be determined. They were very special androids. The technology inside them was revolutionary because of their neural scanning and replicating abilities. A super advanced artificial intelligence designed to first observe and then mimic a human by mapping brain waves and thought patterns, and then anticipating them. They *copied a person.*

The androids in the crate were that project.

John perched in silence with his daughter beside him. He looked upon the android project while a thought percolated. His breath was all that moved, fading away in little puffs of mist. The cold would kill him soon, though he didn't feel it anymore. But that was the joy of hypothermia. He was finally running out of time, his suffering would come to an end at last, and soon.

"Daddy? I have an idea."

Now he needed time. John had forsaken the possibility of his revenge, but these androids were a gift, a blessing, they would see his vengeance fulfilled. He had killed his own children to protect them from the horrors on Space Station Hephaestus, an act that gave John great need for vengeance indeed. Now, ironically, he just needed enough time to get these androids working.

The sewers hid John, providing cover of darkness and sound.

His daughter did not come home. He had sent her to find the next Elite, he never should have sent her. John suffered in darkness through flashbacks of his other kills. He experienced all of the data from his victims. He had terabytes of calculations, and the data played in his head without his permission. Combined with his own emotions, and the emotions of his victims, John didn't know if he could kill again.

John analyzed the street above him from the sewer he was hiding in. There were thirty seven people walking on this street. A lightrail station was seventy two meters northwest.

::Interrupt; Communication protocol initiated::
"John?"

Someone was trying to contact him. It was not his daughter. Where was she? John ignored the attempt to communicate.

"It's Felix. Do you remember me?"

No. Felix was on Hephaestus. Felix was dead. Error:// …John staggered.

I'm dead too! Error://Reboot….

"You sit there and shut the hell up!" Keeb roared. Three accompanying officers disappeared quietly as shadows, Keeb tossed a chair out of his way as he crossed the interrogation room towards Taylor. Taylor had never seen these techniques used from this perspective, he had never been on this side of the interrogation room. It did feel different.

"Sir…"

Commander Keeb clenched the file in his hand as if it were Taylor's neck. "You really know how to *piss me off*!!" he fumed. "A gunfight?! In a cafe?? An *android??*"

"The android was the killer, sir."

Keeb sat on the table's corner, towering above Taylor. He was visibly getting himself under control. Keeb took a brief silence, which garnered Taylor's attention. More than once, and only Taylor would have noticed this, Commander Keeb stopped short of speaking, as if continually changing his mind on what he was about to say. If Taylor didn't know any better, Keeb was struggling with making a decision. "Detective Silas Maheny will now handle this case. You're reassigned, and I need your blaster."

"Silas?!"

"You're going to do what I want from now on, Taylor," Keeb said.

There was an odd confidence in the good Commander's voice now. "Sir?" Taylor asked.

Keeb smiled. "This file, the one in my hands, recognize it? Ever see it before? Want to guess who it's about?"

Taylor stared. He assumed it was another of Keeb's so called suspects.

"It's about you. Interesting stuff, too. So many things I never knew. An orphanage? I didn't know that about you," he stood up and walked back to his seat, letting the silence nestle into Taylor. "You really never knew your parents? How sad. You've been looking for this your whole life I hear."

"So what?"

"So, it's yours now," Keeb said. Taylor didn't understand, and he took a moment to think. Why now? What was so important that Keeb would buy Taylor off like this? And what happened to just getting fired? If Taylor didn't know better he would swear that some powerful person was controlling Commander Keeb, protecting Taylor, a feeling he hadn't been able to shake for days. Partly by the way that no matter what Taylor did, Keeb's response was always far short of what he expected it to be. But Taylor dismissed that notion as quickly as it came. Nothing was out there protecting him, nothing ever had, and nothing ever will.

Reality was, Keeb had him. Taylor's shoulders slouched in defeat. "I let the truth die with that toaster. And in return, you'll give me that file," Taylor said.

"Something like that. But only once this shit storm calms down, and not a moment before," Keeb said, back in control, right where he wanted to be.

Taylor stood up. This wasn't the end he had

expected when he leveled the blaster on that toaster mannequin. This wasn't even close. Taylor plopped his blaster on the table, far harder than necessary. He had other blasters, illegally and otherwise, but the principle of the matter infuriated him. Keeb was going to reassign him? Where, to a desk? Taylor never nodded or verbally agreed, but he didn't need to. Keeb scooped up the blaster and tucked the file safely under his arm before leaving. Truth be told, they both hated each other. Which sort of made Taylor wonder why Keeb ever promoted him in the first place. As Taylor leaned back to soak in his defeat, he made eye contact with the officer that had addressed him earlier, the one who was grateful that Taylor had defied Commander Keeb. Some hero. Taylor was leashed, the defiance dead, Taylor had sold out. And he did it for his birth file.

Over these last few days Taylor had noticed a change in the eyes of his fellow officers. Even the receptionist Jane had smiled at him. At the same time, the badges Taylor knew were attached to Keeb's coattails never let Taylor out of sight. Precinct Four was dividing itself between Taylor's newfound crusade and Commander Keeb's control. He wanted to warn them all to abandon ship.

"A fine mess you've got me in," Taylor said to his reflection in the shower room. Screw it. Give Keeb what he wants. It'll be better that way, just like before. Taylor ducked out, coat tucked under his arm. He couldn't breathe this close to Keeb. He needed to sleep, but the day itself was still young.

Taylor took his walk past the transit station and down the sidewalk towards Pike Place. If he spent another moment hovering on a-grav technology he was going to shoot himself. Besides, a delay from earlier in the day had caused backups throughout the city on all transit routes. Taylor rubbed his sore hands from the chase earlier. Maybe Keeb was right. He just had to give in, and things could be good just like before. What made him think he could take on Keeb anyway? The man's reputation was built upon unworthy adversaries. Taylor could at least say he stopped the *true* killer. The City would never know, the officers would never know, but at least *he* would know. So much for the fame.

Time to celebrate it all away. He always had that. *Bleep. Bleep.*

"Now what?!" Taylor cursed flipping open his telecom. "Detective Taylor speaking."

No response. Taylor checked to see if the call was dead, but it wasn't. Then finally someone spoke.

"Detective. How goes the investigation?"

He knew that voice. Taylor's body tingled from scalp to toes, every hair on his neck hummed in sensation. He knew this voice. Images of the scientist on Fifth Ave flooded in. It was a dead man's voice.

"Who is this??" Taylor demanded.

"We won't refer to myself as a who. We can assume a *what*, after all you were there when he shot himself. *What* is more appropriate. I am a thing, created to finish what my master needed to have finished. I am Persona."

"What is going on??"

"John inspired my creation, actually. Isn't it ironic? His fate became my master's, though this penance was chosen whereas John's was forced. I'm perfected, at least compared to the others. John is, comparably, primitive. It was nice working on the neural technology finally. We've had ten years to work with it," Persona said. His speech patterns were so close to human, but Taylor could sense something missing. He could sense he was talking to a computer.

"You are dead. But… now you are a computer? Did you come back to life? I mean, it's been a long day."

"My original is dead. I'm his persona. I told you this. We'll never get anywhere if I have to repeat myself. There is another murder about to happen."

"Nope. Sorry. You must be behind on current events, I killed your toaster cousin."

"I don't have a body, not like John. No toaster relation, I operate in cyberspace," Persona retorted. For something artificial he seemed touchy.

Taylor blinked. "*Her* name was John? Well, *she's* been deactivated," Taylor said, not liking where this conversation was going. What the hell was a persona? All he wanted to do was go back to following orders. None of this other business was going to help him stay out of trouble.

"Funny thing about androids, Taylor."

Taylor was silent for a long while. A frown had crossed it face, and it stayed there as realization dawned on him. "There's more than one."

"Good! Good. You do catch on."

Taylor didn't want to ask. In fact, he didn't want any part of this. His little deal with Keeb was still fresh in his mind. And it was still his second day without sleep. "Detective Maheny is covering the case now, call him," Taylor said.

"This isn't about him. It's about you. Only you can do something about this," Persona said.

"About what??" Taylor demanded. What about this had anything special to do with Taylor?

"For starters, about stopping the next murder," Persona said.

Taylor closed his eyes, the weight of sleep deprivation weighed on him, despite the late morning sun. He felt his choice long before he said it. "Where is this murder supposed to happen," Taylor finally asked. He kicked himself for asking. The little voice in his head was screaming to hang up and forget everything. He should just throw his phone away, right now, and never look at these murders again.

"John is not easy to track, but I have determined that he's at the old Safeco stadium. And let me warn you, if you had met *him* this morning, they'd be picking up pieces of you instead."

"When?" Taylor asked, walking faster.

"Right now."

Taylor rounded a corner on Third Street, towards Jackson, coincidentally heading in old Safeco Stadium's direction. "Why are you telling me this? Don't you toasters stick together?" Taylor wondered, realizing the convenience of this information. How does Taylor's cooperation help Persona?

"My original created me to end a terrible sin. The real John died long ago, yet his vengeance carries on in purgatory. This is because the very man who killed John is now corrupting John's vengeance. You've heard of him. The leader of New Seattle City."

"Jack Sethren?" Taylor asked. Was that the connection to Sethren Company? Fragmented facts started forming in Taylor's head, like Sethren Tower, the UMA, the Elites, but they would have to wait in the back of his thoughts for now.

"Yes. Jack Sethren. There's much you still don't know, but time is short. Will you let John's manipulated vengeance destroy another innocent life?"

"No...," Taylor answered and hung up. He couldn't talk anymore, something disturbed him, and few things could. It wasn't because someone was about to die, it was the nature of how it was about to happen. The part about vengeance didn't mean much to Taylor, in all honesty. He viewed it as justified violence, usually, the person deserved it. The part about corrupting a man's vengeance, especially by the man who was the reason for that vengeance, was just unforgiveable. Taylor didn't often brush against any morale boundaries, but it was happening now. Old Safeco Stadium was visible by the last piece of that phone call, and it was like stepping into another dimension when the stadium came into view. The stadium was a world away in practice, like a junk drawer in the kitchen full of memories no one wanted, but in reality it was a ten minute walk from the harbor. Old Safeco represented a very dark chapter in the history of the war. By now it was hard to tell which stories about it were true, but all of them were still used to scare kids. Supposedly, Sethren Company was considering renovating it into a war museum.

Persona said he was short on time, and coincidentally Taylor found himself running, unable to cross the distance to the stadium fast enough. Damn the amount of concrete the parking lot took, he felt naked, exposed as he crossed the empty lot, and under every eye in the city. Old Safeco horded light, swallowing it into shadows and grime. Only yellow weeds and a misguided detective occupied the area immediately around it. Safeco's plot rested squarely under what remained of Sears Tower. Safeco used to have a duplicate stadium next to it, but that one did not survive the war. Old Safeco itself was somehow never bombed during the Darkening and because of that, it was soon considered to be a safe zone. A shelter. Refugees flooded to it, hoping to protect their families, thanking the gods for mercy. It was a deliberate rumor, started by someone with a very dark soul. Once the stadium was filled to capacity the doors were sealed. The screams began.

Since the massacre, the retractable roof had never been reopened. Taylor didn't even know if anyone had ever removed the bodies, though he hoped so, especially if he was going inside. Then again, Taylor didn't know *how* he would get inside. And as he stared at one of Safeco's several entrances, taking in the barricades and hastily erected boards, he wondered for a moment if this was where he was supposed to be. Persona didn't specify inside or outside, and Safeco was huge. Taylor craned his head, looking for an inviting spot to try entering. The *old* Taylor wouldn't have cared about any of this, he would have come down here for the fame behind blowing up a killer robot, that's it. Lately, he didn't know which Taylor he was anymore. Taylor clenched his fists. He was the forgetful one, he realized, as he got so mad he almost punched himself. He was here, again, chasing an android, again, without his blaster. Again. *Thanks a lot, Keeb, you dick,* Taylor swore. He wouldn't be unarmed if Keeb hadn't confiscated it.

All of this was wrong. Taylor turned around, wanting to change his mind, but unable to. What happened to laying low? Commander Keeb's deal required him to be silent, to disappear, to stop bringing attention to these happenings. If this came out, at all, he would be throwing away the only chance he had to discover his parents. He pushed his hands through his hair. What would this get him? He needed to be rational for once in his life. He should go back to Precinct Four, and take a nap. Eat a donut. He was removed from the case, after all.

Nuts. Then again, Taylor never was good at following orders.

Keeb's deal died an unremarkable death as Taylor climbed over the concrete barricade and shimmied between two loose wooden boards. No harm in taking a peek.

||Chapter 17||

Taylor peered ahead, seeing only darkness, as he climbed inside. The air was incredibly old, and wet. Sharp wooden splinters stabbed his hands as he climbed between the boards, squeezing in deeper. How did the John robot get in, he wondered. It wasn't this way. Taylor set his foot down, squeezing himself between the barricade, little by little. He went slowly, not because it was so terribly tight, he just didn't want to end up stuck or have something crash down on him. To add to this joy, he had a wet, cold sensation seeping through his shoes. Water had pooled on the ground, probably from clogged storm drains or flooded plumbing. If that was as bad as it got, he was okay with wet feet.

The sounds of the city faded with the light, though there was enough pouring in through slits and cracks to let him see just in front of himself. He cleared the barricade and waited as his ears adjusted to the sudden warp in sound. Dripping water echoed through the vaulted room he was in, it was louder than the city behind him. As his eyes adjusted he saw this was one of the main concession areas, an outer ring of booths circling the arena. Large concrete walls trapped both sides of him, he could go to the left or right, each way totally black. At least he knew why everything echoed so proudly; concrete walls, concrete floor, and he imagined the ceiling very high above him was concrete as well. Carefully, Taylor walked to his left.

He could hear his feet, but he could not see them. He had walked but a meter, and was tempted to light a match for visibility. Not yet. He himself didn't want to be visible, he needed to be here without this John android knowing it. Taylor didn't know if he should think of John as an android or a robot, and he didn't care, they were all fancy toasters to him. Taylor looked behind himself, just to see what little light penetrated the barricade, to remind himself it was there.

Keeping the barricade in sight also helped him keep a sense of direction. So far, he hadn't tripped on anything. He had to wonder, how many happy footsteps carrying drinks and hot dogs took these exact steps so long ago? Only they probably weren't crawling along in the dark. The ghosts in the hallway were making their presence known, Taylor felt every hair on his body standing on end. Not that he believed in such a thing, but darkness like this could make any man superstitious.

    A small beam of light trickled in from the inner arena up ahead. Taylor went towards it, carefully, praying not to step on a dead body, or even a dead rat, or even an empty box. Anything at this point would have made him jump like a little girl. The light came in from his right, from the center of the arena. This was one of the entrances to the seating area, Taylor realized. He rounded the corner and looked in. His view was obstructed by a half set of steps going up, but he could see some of the dome roof. Slowly he walked up the steps, unsure of what to expect, unsure of what he would do if he did see something. At this point, the most he could hope for was a good look at John, unless he found an assault rifle next to one of the seats. The heads of stadium seats created a stunning silhouette, all uniformed and evenly spaced, row by row, facing the arena. Taylor froze, he swore something just brushed by his foot. He looked down just in time to see what might have been a cat, or some large rodent, disappear. He felt a wave of tingles go from head to toe, he really didn't want to be touched by anything. Taylor calmed his pounding chest, and then quickly ducked down. The light was coming from generator powered lamps, down on the field. Standing there, he might have been visible.

    The field was cluttered with large crates overflowing with debris, but luckily there wasn't a mound of charred skeletons. He was happy about that. Taylor wasn't easily spooked, but that would have given him nightmares. From the looks of it, Sethren Company was already somewhere in the renovation process, the equipment on the field belonged to them. Then Taylor saw what he didn't want to see, the reason he had come. In an open clearing on the field, Taylor saw a man bound to a chair with a hood over his face. Standing over him was a very large man in a strange looking construction suit. Taylor took a second look, wondering what he was wearing, and realized that it wasn't really a suit. From here he couldn't get the best look, but Taylor presumed that he was looking at the *John* android.

Persona was right, even from this far away, John looked nothing like the doll faced robot. Even from this distance there was something unnatural about John, something unnerving. Taylor thought about reaching for his blaster, and at the same time remembered how Keeb had confiscated it. All he could do was watch, learn, gather information, and see where this John android went. Which was useless, Taylor decided. The man in the hood wasn't moving anyways. He had no blaster, the victim was dead, John was reasonably terrifying, this was a mistake, and it was a good time to make a quiet exit. He had a nice little adventure sneaking into Safeco, time to get the hell out. He took another look at John. Yep, the doll faced android was one thing, this was another. Reconnaissance be damned, Taylor needed to be armed, heavily.

Then something touched Taylor's leg, again, and this time Taylor jumped. He didn't mean to but he stepped back, tripping over the seat behind him. Taylor fell, grasping for guard rails out of reflex. His clattering echoed, long after he stopped moving. Taylor squeezed his eyes shut. *Stupid! Stupid! Stupid!* If he survived this, he would come back with a flamethrower and do some rodent hunting. Fucking rats! Taylor opened his eyes finally, and when he did, John wasn't standing on the field anymore. Taylor looked for John for half a second until a crash shook him.

He felt it, and certainly heard it, an industrial

sounding crunch, like steel rods driving into concrete. It didn't land right next to him, but it wasn't far away either, the impact resonated through bone and concrete alike. John's silhouette, glowing from the backdrop of light, stood among the line of seats, and Taylor felt his breath escape him. John had leapt from the field to the stadium seats, landing like a boulder. Taylor saw its glowing red eyes, the only part of it that wasn't a silhouette, and they were scanning for him. Taylor shrank behind the row divider, then kept as still as death. He was no longer afraid of that fucking rat. He would curl up next to it if it could hide him. Taylor had been so brave, chasing the doll faced android. He never really thought about how strong she was, despite her jumping through walls and all, subconsciously she just looked like a girl and she ran when he chased. It gave him a sense of power over her. Well, John had destroyed that in a heartbeat. Taylor knew he couldn't just wait and hope. He started to scoot back, his desire to create distance between him and John outweighed his fear of making a sound, especially when John took a step towards him. Carefully he moved his feet back, guiding himself by the base of a hand rail, moving slowly and silently.

Taylor saw John's head was turned to the side and used the opportunity to sneak across the walkway to the lower seating area. He went for it before he had a moment to change his mind in fear, but after darting to the next area he almost wished he hadn't. Taylor was more visible down here, he realized, as light bathed the seats considerably brighter. At least he could see a little better. Taylor stopped and ducked low, the dividing walkway above him was his salvation. He could see John's shoulders, still about twenty meters away, and John was facing in his direction. He needed John to look the other way again so that he could run to the next seating area. Taylor's foot was resting on a piece of wood. He grabbed it, quietly, and considered trying to throw it past John, the old 'look over here' maneuver. Taylor realized that was crazy. This thing wasn't a stupid underpaid security guard. It was the most advanced piece of technology his species had ever created. Still, it was his best bad idea. Taylor pulled his arm back to ready the toss, and before he had to, John's shoulders did an about face. Taylor breathed a sigh of relief, it seemed only fate could keep him from following every stupid thought that he had. Taylor crawled between the seats, ignoring the little squishy pellets he was crushing under his hands and knees. Rat droppings. He definitely wanted to come back with a flamethrower now. Taylor heard John walking, but the echo made it too difficult to tell if he was coming closer or going further away. Taylor froze, waiting, wishing, wondering.

After a few quiet moments Taylor risked looking over the line of seats again, John's head was still turned the other way. If he was lucky, John was following the rat that started all of this. If he was doubly lucky, John had a flamethrower for a hand and was going to cook the son of a bitch for him. Taylor scooted further away from John, keeping low, trying to dodge the debris that increasingly littered the space between stadium seats. And if it wasn't for a very round steel pipe, he might have been able to low-crawl his way all the way out of there. But when his foot accidentally nudged the heavy pipe, it rolled, and fell, and clattered as loudly as it possibly could, for as long as it possibly could. Taylor was on his feet and running in the next instant.

He felt John coming after him, and without taking the time to think about it, he just knew he could never outrun it. He saw the field down below and sprinted that way, because he could go faster downhill. It sounded like a great plan to Taylor as he ran for the ledge, though the field itself didn't offer any particular security. He knew it would prolong his chances by a few seconds, and as far as survival instincts went, that was surviving. He sprinted down the steps and leapt for the ledge, springing off of the guard rail, and aimed for a storage crate not far below. If he was real lucky, it might be full of soft insulation.

Taylor flew, fast, the feeling of weightlessness consumed him until the fear of landing took over. His heel caught the rim of the storage crate, and he tumbled in. His head came to rest almost but not quite touching the unforgiving steel wall of the crate, just an inch further and Taylor's brain would have been bleeding all over it. He landed on a mess of planks and long, not sharp materials, for which Taylor was very grateful. And as soon as he had his wind back, he highly intended to start running again. It all happened so fast that if he knew what he had landed on, he would probably be wincing in pain. He had to thank shock and adrenaline for those small gifts. Taylor gritted his teeth, trying to prop himself up. No, he wasn't going to be running anytime soon. Taylor yanked a pipe loose from underneath him and managed to sit up.

"Alright you nasty little toaster, I can't run anymore," Taylor said, tipping his body over the side of the crate. He fell onto the ground indelicately, taking the pipe with him. He climbed back to his feet, hefting the pipe, which was wieldy in a way that he liked. "Let's go, bitch," Taylor wheezed. He held the pipe, expecting John to just pummel him that instant. But that didn't happen, he didn't even see John, and after a second Taylor limped towards the man in the chair, mostly because it had the most light and was a better position. When he got there, he couldn't see much of the stadium in the distance, but he could feel it. He felt it as if it were full of eyes, all looking down on him.

"What are you waiting for?" Taylor shouted, wielding his pipe like a bat. Then he saw John, standing there, his red eyes shining somewhere near the edge of a baseball diamond. Taylor resisted the urge to run away. He needed what little radius of light there was, and he could not fight in the dark. The profile of John's frame came into the light. Taylor reshuffled his feet.

"Come on!!" he shouted. John came at him, crossing the distance in a second. Taylor stepped to the side and swung the pipe, aiming for a homerun.

Thwack!

The pipe shot off of John's skull, the residual jolt bit back like a bolt of lightning. John was frozen on his feet, dazed, hopefully having a meltdown. Despite the pain in his forearms Taylor swung the pipe again. John came to and dodged, however, and the pipe swung harmlessly through the air. John stepped in and grabbed Taylor's neck, picking him up with one hand. He held Taylor there, suspended by his neck, his steel fingers about to crush his throat.

"Do it already!" Taylor whispered as robotic fingers clutched his neck. Taylor was surprised at himself, surprised that he was so ready to die. Earlier, when there was a chance to live, survival instincts took over. But now, with a robotic hand about to crush his throat, he was face to face with himself. No bravado, no pretend machismo, Taylor was ready. His life was without meaning, he had suffered almost every day of his existence, and he welcomed not knowing that pain anymore. So, what was it waiting for?

Then John relaxed his grip ever so slightly. Its head went limp, literally as if shutting down. Taylor took in a welcome breath of air and struggled to free himself from John's hand. What happened? A malfunction? Did Taylor manage to break something inside its head? Suddenly John's head popped up and he grabbed Taylor by the arm. Taylor cried out from sudden, intense pain.

"I can't kill you," John said. "But I can hurt you," he added, and then ripped Taylor's arm off.

John disappeared into the dark as Taylor lay on the ground. He couldn't hear anything, thanks to shock, and then he couldn't see anything. He tried to call someone, but his arm wasn't working. No, it was gone. The stadium was spinning, with Taylor at the center. He brought his hand to his face, hoping to stop the spinning. In a moment of clarity

Taylor used his chin to activate his telecom, but he didn't know if he actually managed to call anyone by the time he passed out. After days of no sleep, fighting two robots, and having his arm ripped off, his body had enough.

　　　　Jack Sethren paced, struggling to bury the rage that had overflowed moments before. Members of his staff, the ones he had ordered out in a furious outburst, were all afraid he was about to fire them all. No. He had come very close to killing them all. And it was because of Taylor.

　　　　Like an idiot, Taylor had gone after the John android, and most surprisingly, someone had helped him. And then it almost killed Taylor. It almost ruined everything Jack Sethren had waited so long for. Thankfully, gratefully, the programming Felix installed had held, programming that kept the John android from killing Taylor. Fuck if he shouldn't have been more specific about not hurting him either.

　　　　Luckily for a countless number of souls that would have suffered Jack Sethren's wrath, his recovery crew found Taylor in time and admitted him into a first class medical center. Jack Sethren was only able to contain his rage because after all irreducible facts, his plan had not failed. He had a close call, for certain, but all was not lost. Someone was helping Taylor, someone who would regret that mistake for every last moment of their life, but his plan was still alive, it would still work. He rested his head against a marble pillar, alone in his suite, comprising the top few floors of Sethren Tower.

　　　　His revenge was finally coming to an end.

||Chapter 18||

"Ms Payer? Are you home?" Taylor called. Today was Taylor's thirteenth birthday and Ms Payer had asked him to stop by after school. He had a feeling she made him a cake. Taylor was just glad she remembered his birthday. She was the only one.

"Hello-oo?" Taylor tried again. Her lights were on, kitchen utensils strewn about, a mixing spoon moist with cake batter, bowls and ingredients fresh on the counter, yet an overwhelming burnt smell clogged the air. Taylor quickly shut off the oven and inspected the cake inside. It was charred black.

"I think the cake is done, Ms Payer, hehe," Taylor joked nervously.

Taylor fidgeted with his shirt. Did she leave? Something felt odd.

Taylor walked down the hall to the bedroom. Perhaps she fell asleep waiting for the cake to finish. He tapped softly on the door hoping he wasn't intruding. Another burning smell came from the room, and it was not cake. Taylor pushed open the door.

Ms Payer's room was empty, but the smell was terrible. He stepped two paces into her bedroom and froze by the bathroom door. Water flooded out of her tub. He saw her hand resting limp along the porcelain. Taylor rushed over to turn off the water but pops and crackles of electricity stopped him.

He saw Ms Payer's naked body, her kitchen blender in her hands shooting out sparks, a handwritten note taped to the mirror. Taylor never ran so fast in his life.

Three weeks later he sat in class, he hadn't missed a single day of school. The orphanage did not forgive truancy. It was Mr. Klein, who gave the most forgettable lessons in algebra, who pulled him out of his trance with a simple question.

"What is your problem, Taylor? You've been in a daze for weeks now."

"Me?" Taylor replied, and then fell silent. He seemed to be unable to speak. When he finally looked up, with defeated eyes, the teacher was unable to ask him anything further. Taylor never did answer the question. Whatever had happened to Taylor, it wasn't going to be said, ever.

Floating through space. Still alive. "Daddy, when are you coming home?"

John didn't feel cold anymore. In outer space and without heat he knew he did not have long to live. But he had to finish. This was his only chance to get back at the ones who did this to him and his family. "I'm almost done working, honey. How was school today?"

"Good daddy, I did my homework."

John wasn't thinking. She couldn't go to school from here. They were trapped in a cargo lock drifting in space.

"Daddy... do I still have to drink this?"

"Stop!!" John yelled. She disappeared, she always disappeared when he yelled. John didn't have much time, he kept working. She was dead. She was dead because he had killed her. He had killed her to protect her. The poison in the juice was a merciful death. As her father, he couldn't let the terrible, unspeakable things happen to her that were coming. Why did he have to make that terrible choice? WHY?!

"I'm sorry about yelling at you, honey. I'm almost done. I'm coming home soon! I promise..."

John's mind was so clear now, not like before.

Ironically, so close to death, he could see things so well.

"Mommy misses you."

"I know, honey. I'm almost done."

"Daddy?"

"Yes, little miss?"

"Their eyes are glowing. Are they on now? The androids?"

"Yes, yes! We did it!"

And John's vengeance had new life. The androids memorized him, copied him, carefully absorbed each of his warped brainwaves, adopted them as their own, and carried on John's spirit when his body failed. And because John had so heavily hallucinated his daughter, the second android became her, or at least, it became the way John knew her.

Hospitals have for all time possessed a unique smell that is unbearable. A sterilized, waterless discomfort. The smell was what woke Taylor up, and that's when he knew. When he looked over, his right arm was gone. His arm ended in the middle of the bicep, bandaged in layers. And he was drugged, heavily drugged, because it was fun to turn his head left and right. Taylor had really hoped it was all a bad dream. He wasn't angry yet, but it was coming. He knew himself too well for it not to.

When Taylor opened his eyes he half expected Vina would be there, or Catheri, waiting patiently. But no one was waiting for Taylor's recovery. Instead he was greeted by medical monitors and cables hooked onto his chest, whatever the hell they were for. The rest of the room was actually quite nice, if he cared about such things. "Hello?!" Taylor yelled, his head pounding instantly. This was a private recovery room. He was very surprised Precinct Four would pay for it, Detective or not. From his bed he had a nice view of the city, only the tops of aged skyscrapers broke the amber sky. The early rays of sunlight gleamed, or, they were the last rays of the day. He didn't know yet, and it hurt trying to decide. One thing he wondered, how did he get here?

No nurses or medical staff had responded to him yet. Taylor saw a television remote next to him and turned it on, just to feel some company. The far side of his room had a lounge area full of plush chairs. Well, at least if he had visitors, they would be able to sit somewhere. He could be staying in a hotel if not for the medical equipment. He changed channels until he found the weather. There was a slight chance of rain, so he knew he was still in New Seattle City. What a relief, except Taylor was far too anxious to relax. The room was just too nice, and no one was here to explain why he was here instead of in a shitty basic hospital recovery room. Maybe the hospital staff got him confused with someone else, someone more important. Taylor finally noticed a call button and pressed it. How did he get here? He wished he could remember.

"Good morning Detective, how are you today?" a woman's soft voice answered.

Taylor rolled his eyes. "I'm hungry, thirsty, ahh, a slight itch in my ass, what do you think?! I'm missing my arm, bitch!" And there he was. Taylor showed up, as soon as there was someone to be a dick to.

"I'll send someone to your room, sir."

Taylor laughed. Now he knew there was a mistake, because moments later someone did come to his room, and they brought a rolling cart loaded with appetizers and a chilled bottle of Colombian Chardonnay.

"You brought wine. Is this a farewell to arms party?"

The server did not answer, young and clean shaven, he set the cart next to Taylor in an awkward silence and then wished him a pleasant day before leaving. Taylor, still wondering what kind of mistake this was, inspected the cart. He saw cooked asparagus, artichokes, colored cheeses, and some green herbs he could not name. Instantly his mouth watered. This wasn't normal hospital food. And Keeb would never have paid for this. But, there wasn't a mistake made that Taylor wasn't willing to capitalize on. He grabbed the rim of the cart with his left arm and pulled it closer, scooped a handful of buttered asparagus, and devoured it. He had to be very deliberate about eating with one hand, and patient. The first time he tried to wipe glistening oil off his chin with his right arm, as if it had magically reappeared, he almost lost it. The second time he tried to, he hurled a plate full of asparagus bits across the room. For awhile, he watched the plate on the floor, in silence except for the television. He knew what his problem was, he was weak now. He hated that. He would need a left-handed blaster, a big one. He would also need to get informed on cybernetics, find out what his prosthetic options would be. But, he wasn't ready to think that far ahead. He was still processing the fact that his arm was torn off by a killer robot.

Taylor grabbed a fried oyster from the tray, it was cooked with pieces of bacon and smelled incredible. He crammed it in his mouth and wondered why he was taking this so well, and then pushed the cart tumbling over. Appetizers and utensils spilled across the floor, the crate clattered as its contents hit the deck. The chardonnay bottle lay on its side, casually spilling itself, aromatically bubbling into the carpet. He reached for the phone near his bed and dialed, realizing just now that the staff put everything on his left side for convenience.

"Communications."

"Let me talk to Catheri," Taylor said. While he was on hold he set the phone down and leaned over the side to grab another bacon fried oyster off the ground. He was still hungry. He figured he had half a second before Catheri answered the phone, so he stuffed the oyster in his mouth.

"Detective Taylor's office," Catheri said.

"MM-hhmm," he muttered, trying to chew his mouthful.

"Taylor? Is that you?" Catheri asked.

Swallow. "Yeah," swallow again, "it's me. Do you miss me yet?"

"Every *inch* of you. Where are you?"

Now Taylor was really surprised. The precinct didn't know where he was? This was definitely a mistake, in his favor of course. "I'm on my way. Can you get me a left-handed blaster? A big one?"

"What? Why?" she asked. Taylor looked across the room for a moment and decided he wasn't ready to answer that question. Instead he hung up the phone and leaned over the bed for the half full bottle of chardonnay. He didn't need a glass.

Taylor's clothes were cleaned, mended, and hanging in the closet of his room. They were not the clothes that he had come in. Someone brought a set of his clothes here, but Catheri didn't know where he was? Maybe it was Vina, but trying to think of how that all worked hurt his head. Taylor undid the wires monitoring him, dressed in his clean clothes with his left hand, stuffed many more bites of food, and drank more wine. Getting dressed was difficult. His pants were easier than his shirt, as he kept trying to use both hands on the buttons. Once he was dressed he noticed a bottle full of pain meds was sitting near his nightstand, he pocketed it as he walked out the room.

The hallway outside was warmly colored with oak browns and a vibrant, red carpet runner. He really was in a hotel, aside from the stale medical equipment. A middle aged receptionist waited near the elevator, and she smiled at him. She had a truthful look about her. He stopped there, placing his hand casually on the counter.

"Hey, where can I pay the bill for my room?"

"Don't you work for Sethren Co.?" she replied.
Taylor almost swallowed, but managed not to. Was it still
coincidence?

"Of course I do. Thanks," Taylor said as he walked
off. This didn't feel like some kind of administrative typo
anymore, but his head was swimming too much to even
attempt thinking about it right now. He had the worst kind
of hangover. Taylor could only focus on pressing the
elevator button with his left hand and standing up straight.
He didn't realize how much pain medication he was on until
he got on the elevator, the subtle adjustments in the floor
made him terribly unstable. He reached out to grab the
support rail with his missing arm and fell against the elevator
wall, waiting for it to stop. It was just a normal elevator
going down.

He left the hotel lobby, and indeed as he walked out
he remarked that it was a *hotel*. A hotel with a special floor
reserved for first class Citizens requiring luxury medical
care. Secluded from regular guests, filled with medical staff
and equipment specially reserved for the wealthy. A typo?
No, not anymore. This was connected, it all was, but he
didn't know how. Why would Sethren Company pay for his
medical treatment? Especially when he was uncovering so
many buried, dark secrets about their top level staff? It
didn't make sense to Taylor. He should have woken up in
Safeco, in pain, alone, if he woke up at all. Which was
another question. Before it happened, John said he couldn't
kill Taylor. Why the hell not?

That was a question for Persona. Taylor had to get
to the office and find a way to contact him.

When he boarded the lightrail he half expected to
run into someone he knew and be forced to explain his arm.
At the moment he would just reply, "What arm?" but he
doubted that would be enough to satisfy Catheri. Along the
way he continued to attempt to use his right hand; when his
nose itched, to flick paper off his seat, to adjust his hair.

When he finally entered the lobby of Precinct Four he just
walked in with his jacket hanging limp on one side, and
proceeded all the way to his office eventually shutting the
door behind him. Catheri was the first to notice, not
surprisingly, leaping from her chair and spitting out her
coffee mid sip.

"What happened?! Shit Taylor, your arm!"
"What arm?"

"Taylor, ...look at your arm, you... yesterday your
face, and now your *arm*?!"

"I fell." But he didn't fall, and he was ready to
throw something if she didn't shut up about it already.

"How can you joke about this??" she cried. She
reached out at Taylor's missing limb, as if touching it would
make it real to her, but he jerked away. Catheri put her
hands to her face in disbelief. "I need a minute," she said
before disappearing into the hallway. Taylor walked into his
office and took a look before coming back to Catheri's
office. He didn't see a left-handed blaster anywhere, maybe
she thought he was joking earlier. Well, she probably
believed him now. She stepped back in the room a moment
later, a very forced calm on her face.

Taylor chose to speak first. "I'll get it fixed, good as
new. Did you find me that left handed blaster?"

"Yes, though at the moment I'm certain I don't want
you to have it."

"Wouldn't hit anything with it anyway, I'm a terrible
lefty." It was easy for him to joke, but Taylor was far more
pissed off than he sounded. He was angry, angry about his
arm, angry about getting his ass kicked by John, angry about
being a fool for running blindly into something, angry about
listening to mysterious tips from a dead man's software. He
just needed to go see the doctor again, get fixed up, and get
on with it. Catheri shook her head. A note lay on the table.
Taylor snatched it up, eager to hear from Persona, but

instead it was from Commander Keeb.

CALL WHEN YOU GET THIS

Taylor shut his eyes, clenching the note in his hand. What the hell did he want now? He looked at the calendar and almost gasped. It had been two days? He lost two days? And he still had a job? Hours at a time he might disappear from duty, be hard to reach, be unaccountable. But days? Catheri was used to Taylor disappearing, but Keeb's new Detective had to have a shorter leash than this. At least, Taylor had assumed as much.

Taylor disappeared into his office and paced. Catheri was on the phone shortly, probably asking a doctor if she could surgically donate her right arm to him. Taylor looked around his room, hoping to find another note. He checked his phone, but Persona hadn't called. He needed to get a hold of him, before anything else moved. Taylor needed to know why John didn't kill him, and why Sethren Company saved him. And he needed to know before talking to Commander Keeb. If he was going to give up this investigation, for his birth file or any other reason, he had to have answers to those questions if nothing else. Taylor plopped into his chair, leaned back and closed his eyes.

Catheri walked in the room. With his eyes closed, Taylor could feel her trying to lighten the mood. She was terrible at it. "Well, you are becoming a bit more popular around the Precinct. Everyone is talking about you. And some of it isn't bad," Catheri said.

"That's nice," Taylor said, reaching for the vodka in the desk. Catheri stepped forward to claim Taylor's attention back.

"Just let it go, the case, all of it, do it for *us,*" she said, suddenly serious and pleading with him. Taylor had never seen her so worried. It took him aback for a moment.

"I can't. I'm sorry." Taylor sort of regretted saying it. He had nothing to be sorry for.

"But Taylor, Keeb told you to back off," she begged. She must have expected him to reply that way, knowing the personal touch 'for *us*' would be a long shot with him.

"Keeb can kiss my ass." Maybe it was the drugs, the disoriented feeling he had since waking up, but Taylor realized that his door had opened just as he said that. And when he looked, he realized it was Commander Keeb standing there.

"You must have missed the message ordering you to contact me right away," Keeb said, appearing. "Doubtless you knew I was standing here. Are you missing an arm?" He meant that, it was a genuine surprise.

"What arm?" Taylor said.

Catheri nervously straitened her dress as if it was plotting her death. "Commander I was just coming to call you--"

"Would you excuse us, Catheri," Taylor said motioning his left hand to the door.

"Oh no, don't let me interrupt. Now, Taylor, what were you saying?"

Taylor peered up at Keeb, he was well past any stage where he could be intimidated. Compared to John, Keeb was nothing.

"I was saying that *I'm* the new Detective for Precinct Four, this is *my* case, and I have a suspect," Taylor said. "Then I said you can kiss my ass."

Keeb's face turned a shade of crimson and then purple. "Taylor, I scheduled you an appointment with the psychiatrist. You are obviously under duress," he said with great difficulty. Something was holding him back! Keeb's face was two shades away from merlot, and he was recommending a psychiatrist? The terrible Commander Keeb of Precinct Four? Taylor had nothing to fear now.

"No time sir, I've got to catch another robot. You know, after you blow one away it just gets addicting," Taylor said.

Blush and eyeliner were the only colors left on

Catheri's ghostly face. During the conversation she had inched closer and closer towards the door. No one disrespected Commander Keeb. It was as if she were afraid of being caught in the blast.

Keeb finally burst, he swept the top of Taylor's desk off and grabbed Taylor by the shirt. But that was it. After a long stare, he tossed Taylor back to his seat, smoothing out his hair and shirt. Taylor winced from the jolt. Catheri gripped the door handle like it was a life vest.

"Stay Catheri, Keeb wants you to," Taylor reminded her.

"It's *Commander* Keeb, *Detective* Taylor. And you will show me all respects due," his voice shaking. Whatever was holding Commander Keeb back just became Taylor's greatest interest. Maybe it was just his young detective instincts, but Sethren Company came to mind. They saved him once already.

An ounce of pride reentered Commander Keeb. Whatever was controlling him, Taylor recognized it was doing so just barely. "I warn you, no one is safe from me," he said, so low Taylor almost didn't hear it. Keeb left without another word or so much as a glance. Catheri remained frozen with her eyes wide and mouth shut, no color had returned to her face. She wouldn't make a peep, so Taylor filled in the silence.

"Catheri, how about that left-handed problem solver?"

Catheri didn't hear him. She was waiting to make sure Keeb was nowhere nearby. Taylor watched her for a moment, wondering if that display of dick sizing was really so traumatic for her. Finally she moved, kicked the door with her heel and bit her lip. She was gathering the resolve to say something.

"Stupid, stupid, stupid," she repeated. She started pacing the room and then Taylor couldn't take anymore.

"Okay, what the hell did you do?"

Catheri looked up at the heavens before spilling

what was on her mind. "Taylor, I stole this, it's from Keeb's office. I haven't looked at it yet," she said and revealed a file, it was Taylor's birth file.

"Who else knows about this," he asked.

"No one, obviously. Please Taylor, I did it for you. I mean, I did it for us," she grabbed him and kissed him, pulling his face in with both hands.

Taylor waited until she was done, it was the least he could do. But his eyes were open, staring at the file on his desk.

Chapter 19

There was a page in his file that Taylor had stared at for almost an hour. The page where somebody had to sign for him, the day he was delivered to the orphanage. Justin Spiel. Taylor stared at it, already knowing it was a fake name. But he wasn't looking at the name, he was looking at the ink, at the indentation on the paper, at the spot where someone signed him away as a baby. He was seeing the only physical connection to his beginning, and it was through this worthless piece of paper. When he finally flipped from front to back, sorting redundant documents, orphanage papers, the stamp that said 'anonymous' again and again, he felt betrayed. He literally couldn't move, worse than being kicked in the nuts. Nothing was listed. All he had was the imprint of that pen on a piece of paper. For as much time as he had spent coveting this file, he almost laughed at how useless it was.

When he no longer felt sick, he actually found himself a little relieved. He had spent so much time and energy looking for that stupid file, for nothing. And thanks to Catheri's foolishness, Taylor wouldn't be swayed by its omniscient aura anymore. To hell with Keeb's deal. In the end, so what if he knew anything about his parents. What would it change? Taylor set the file away from him, to the furthest part of his desk. He suddenly couldn't stand to be near it.

Taylor stood. There was something else that Catheri finally brought him, and it would prove to be more important than that cursed file. The left-handed blaster. He flung the thing across the room the first time he tried to quick-draw, and after cursing himself he snatched it off the floor to try again. And again. And again. He pushed himself, drawing the blaster over and over. But no matter how hard he pushed, how deeply he insulted himself, he couldn't draw it as fast as his natural right hand did. At least he stopped throwing it across the room. The matching holster fit under his right stump where his arm used to be. There was only one trick that seemed to help make it feel natural, and that was when he pretended he was holding two guns, one in each hand. Taylor hadn't looked at the prosthetic selections available to him yet. He was too afraid that they would be so pathetically below what he could accept that it would reopen this emotional wound. He wasn't ready for disappointment right now.

Taylor was determined, albeit self punishing. Now that he knew who, or what, he was tracking, he knew how to prepare. He didn't have all the puzzle pieces, he didn't know the whole story yet, especially the part that had to do with him. But he at least knew how to prepare for John. He needed firepower. The rest of the details would come, and if it didn't, so what. He didn't need to know every dirty little secret about Sethren Company and its genocidal employees. He would keep it simple and find the killer, John. But he couldn't find John without Persona. Of course, he didn't actually know how to find Persona, either.

Taylor didn't feel safe operating out of his office, not until he knew more about what was holding Keeb back. Not to mention, he had spent far too much time behind the walls of Precinct Four. So he went to the sidewalks outside in search of an old fashioned *cybercafé*, both for coffee, and to raise some networking alarms. He hoped in doing so, Persona would find him. It was Friday, the last day of the workweek. He noticed more musicians playing on the streets on Fridays, without ever wondering why. Not that he was about to start, he hated street musicians. Taylor trudged up a steep sidewalk from Third to Fourth St. Shopping stores were on this block, but he knew that before reading any signs, simply inhaling told him so. The array of perfumes on this block, especially if you caught the wind just right, could make your wife think you were the cheating type. Luckily before taking too much time in this part of town he found the place he was looking for and stepped inside. *Red Roost,* a coffee house with locally roasted red coffee beans, whatever that meant. He imagined the name was meant to add a country style appeal to the place, but Taylor knew what was beyond those city walls, and there was nothing romantic about that apocalyptic wasteland.

"I need coffee," he said to the barista with spiky hair. "Cream and sugar."

In moments Taylor held an oversized mug, careful not to spill, and sat down in front of a dated CRT monitor and computer. As archaic as the technology was, it still worked. Since tech factories were only now finding their feet, production of electronics was dodgy. Technology was catching up with its former self, but it had far to go before androids like John were ever made again. Taylor took a sip from his coffee, analyzing what he was about to do. He didn't know how to find Persona, but he knew he could *be* found if he tried, and if someone was looking. Taylor took another sip and set the coffee down, wondering what kind of risk he was about to take, and opened a networking program.

[[INTERFACE: find Sethren Co. Host]]

The software connected to servers and hosts and ran into a big, ugly red warning against unauthorized users. It did look intimidating, Taylor noted. Most people should really heed those warnings, he thought to himself. Then Taylor started pressing buttons.

[[ENTER LOGON: ... Felix]]
[[LOGON DENIED]]

Naturally it wasn't going to be that easy, but when poking a hornet's nest, you just keep poking. He figured he would be red flagged somewhere if he kept typing in things that people were being killed over. Taylor typed everything he could think of. He entered John, Jack Sethren, Taylor, Keeb, Phonm, Kayd, Android, Toaster... nothing was showing any immediate response. Taylor typed in *Cargo Lock 5,* and a blip appeared onscreen.

[[You are making this difficult.]]

"Time for you to fill in the blanks," he said, hoping this was Persona.

[[Not now detective, John was looking for you, and I think he just found you, thanks to your carelessness. Your police are coming here too, for John… I don't know how they got here so fast, unless they were tipped off. This can't be good. You are out of time, you must leave. Immediately.]]

"Why didn't John kill me?"

[[Because we programmed him not to. Now go. Right now.]]

"What? Why? What do I have to do with anything?!"

[[Thirty seconds. They are here. If you survive this I will contact you--]]

[[…END SESSION]]

Taylor was rereading everything when the windows shook from incoming aerial assault vehicles. At first he thought he must be near a crime in progress, subconsciously ignoring Persona's repeated warnings. Then Taylor realized that *he* was the crime in progress. Assault vehicles? He had several simultaneous questions, such as why, and how. Assault vehicles didn't mount up because someone was hacking Sethren Company. Taylor had missed the direness of Persona's warnings, otherwise he would have been long gone by now. He and Persona obviously needed to work out a few miscommunication issues. Taylor stood, accidentally knocking his coffee off the table, and looked for the quickest way out of here.

Through the window he saw AGV, Air-Ground-Vehicles, landing on the sidewalk as two Cruisers ripped to a halt. A team of Heavily Armored Ground, HAGs, formed positions to storm the cafe. For him? This was as overkill as his infamous Crawler assault. Taylor couldn't be more confused, all he did was fiddle on the computer! Either way, he definitely wasn't going out the front door. Taylor ducked into the back prep area and headed for the alleyway exit. Just as Taylor went to open the back door, he paused as it opened for him, ready to flash his badge and talk his way out of here. But he realized that wouldn't work, and also that the HAG unit wasn't here for Taylor. They were here for something else. Persona had warned Taylor that John found him, now Taylor knew what he meant by that.

John ripped into the back of the café, and Taylor spun on his heels, running before his feet had traction. All at once adrenaline propelled him, the kind of adrenaline that makes prey feel nothing before it is eaten. Taylor felt like a witness to what happened next rather than part of it.

John grabbed Taylor and threw him to the floor. The HAG unit blew the door down with a wall splitter, shattering the side windows. Blaster rounds lit up the lobby, cindering particles floated in the air from shredded table cloths and napkins. John toppled the first HAG that came inside. Taylor drew his left handed blaster and blew open John's knee.

John crashed like a slab of granite. Taylor aimed for John's head. John rolled as Taylor fired, the round ricocheted off John's shoulder. Taylor backpedaled, bumping tables and chairs as he tried to fire one armed to stop John from reaching him.

A shower of sparks filled the room. Taylor collapsed under an electronet, a non lethal riot control weapon. It blanketed John and Taylor both, he was pinned to the floor as if a piano fell on him though it was little more than a pattern of intricate wires. The HAG unit stormed in and surrounded them. Taylor forced his head to turn under the electronet and locked eyes with John. There were human eyes staring back at him, full of emotion. Taylor felt pity for those eyes before he blacked out from the electric shock.

"Detective!"

Taylor awoke, he was off the floor and propped in a cafe chair. A medic was applying a blood pressure cuff, Commander Keeb towered nearby. The android still lay on the floor under the electronet, a stretcher was being slid under it. He looked much more like a robot when frozen to the ground than the human it thought it was. Taylor's head rang, he must have bumped it collapsing to the floor. Keeb took more than a few glances at John, everyone did. John was the forgotten past and coming future, all in one.

"Wrap this up. Get that thing loaded. Spiel, Grolsch, get on media detail. Where's the barista?" Keeb barked. Taylor watched Keeb for a moment before it completely sank in; nobody was here to arrest Taylor. Taylor could have laughed, or kicked himself. He was so self-centered. Persona told him the police were coming for John, and he still assumed they were after him, because he's so damn important. Ha! It was laugh worthy, Taylor had to admit it. He shrugged the medic away and stood from his chair as the HAG unit readied to pick up the android. He wasn't under arrest, which meant he was technically working now. Taylor scooted in to help them lift, even if it was just with one arm. He had one chance to take advantage of this before John disappeared to a lab somewhere.

Taylor helped carry John and his stretcher carefully through the cafe and into the back of a holding van. No one questioned him, no one even glanced twice at Taylor. When John's frame was all but secured into the back of the van, Taylor looked around to see who was within earshot. "I'm riding alone in the back with it. Keeb's orders," Taylor lied.

"Aren't we waiting for Commander Keeb?" Officer Spiel asked. The other HAG officers were milling at the back of the van, waiting to be told what to do next. Stupid Spiel, always too nosy.

"You know how he loves the media, he said for us to go without him," Taylor lied again. Taylor climbed in back and a HAG tried to climb in with him.

"This *tech* is classified above your pay grade, sorry," Taylor said, waving his hand out to stop him. The HAG nodded and backed away. When the doors shut it was just Taylor and John. The dim light and sudden quiet brought back images of Safeco, of his arm being ripped off, and Taylor felt his body responding in a post traumatic way. Strange, how even secured to the stretcher, with the thickest straps the precinct had, John could cast fear in Taylor. Taylor studied him, surrounded by the background ambience of a police scene. This thing had tried to kill him once, but it was programmed not to, and there had to be a reason. The lights behind its eyes came on. Taylor held the button to the electronet in his hand, ready to zap John still again.

"Can you speak?" Taylor asked.

John looked at him, his eyes glowing softly behind glass retinas.

"Yes."

Taylor let out his breath. "Why wouldn't you kill me?"

John did not reply. If his mechanical eyes were any indication, he might not really know.

"Fair enough," Taylor said and thought for a moment. He asked the one thing he could think of. "What is Cargo Lock 5?"

John looked long and hard for a moment, and his voice changed. "I think I died there," he remarked. Taylor said nothing until John spoke again. "They made me do it, but I got them back. I *made* them feel what I felt, I *made* them do what I did. I only have to kill once more."

"Who?"

"Colonel Jack Sethren, the leader of the assault on Space Station Hephaestus."

Taylor pulled the left handed blaster out and pressed the muzzle into John's forehead.

"What are you feeling right now?"

"I have to make him pay."

"Yeah, we'll get back to that." Taylor sat back down. John was making less sense now, and his voice changed from the emotional person to the emotionless robot.

"Felix is talking to me, but he's dead."

"What?" Taylor asked.

John's voice softened again, a simple metamorphosis that changed everything about the way Taylor saw him. Suddenly he was a person again. "We were on the space station when they found us. Elites were killing everyone, I wouldn't let them kill my children. I wouldn't let them be butchered, so I protected them. My children died in peace. I was supposed to die too. Maybe I did. But I'm still here. Jack is the last one---" Taylor watched as John convulsed gently, as if there was some error in his programming. The van they were in finally started and sped away, just as Taylor could hear Keeb calling for anyone who knew where Detective Taylor was. For a moment, Taylor wondered what John meant when he said his children died in peace. If the Elites were coming, brutal murderers that they were, how did his children die in peace? Then Taylor realized what he meant, and it made him sick to his stomach.

"I don't want to kill anymore. Kayd, Phonm, they deserved to suffer, but I can't take anymore," John shook softly. It took Taylor a moment to realize that it was *trying* to cry. This was a far different John than the destroyer that attempted to kill him earlier. This John really thought it was a human.

"John, it's okay. You don't have to worry about that now," Taylor said. He knew of the Elites, everyone did, and he didn't need John to elaborate to understand the rest. In whatever crazy way it happened, John was a real person once, not an android. Felix's cryptic words and Persona's riddles told about a great sin, and Taylor realized now John was that sin. What John did to his children, what they made him do, was that sin. And this robot was John's vengeance, forcing the former Elites to do as John had done, to murder their own loved ones, to protect them from the hell John would bring down on them. Taylor drooped his head. What the hell happened on Space Station Hephaestus?

John had faded out, so Taylor tapped John's chest. His eyes opened, he was a person again, confused by his surroundings. Taylor rested his hand gently on John's shoulder, he found himself closing his eyes. John wasn't the monster he thought he was. "You deserve peace, John. Why did you come after me? Why did you take my arm?"

John visibly relaxed. "I did it to hurt Jack Sethren."

A chuckle escaped Taylor. In what universe did Taylor have anything to do with Jack Sethren? It wasn't like Jack Sethren was his father. Society was many things these days, but it was not morally crippled, at least not openly. A public figure like Jack Sethren could never illegitimately father a child. And if he did, it would be a well kept secret.

A small little voice in Taylor's head started to laugh. Abandoned at an orphanage, that's one way to hide a secret. And what would Jack Sethren do when Taylor grew up? Like a dad he would pave the way for him, get him a cush job somewhere. It made sense now why Taylor was promoted to Detective without any qualifications, and why Keeb would never make good on his threats, and why he awoke in a first class recovery room. If Jack Sethren was his dad then he was somewhere in the background pulling the strings. Taylor released the safety on the blaster. Of all the dads he could have had... The little voice in Taylor's head was roaring with laughter.

"I'm speaking to John now, are you listening? What do you really want?"

"... I just want to be with my family..."

"John, go be with them now."

The shot blasted through his metallic skull casing, the soft glowing lights behind the glass eyes disappeared. John's tormented soul could finally be at peace.

]]Chapter 20[[

Taylor bounced off the inside wall as the van screeched to a halt. He climbed over John and unlatched one of John's bindings. A second later the rear hatch door flew open with two rifle muzzles aimed inside, ready to obliterate. Taylor held his hand in the air above his head, his right stump nudged slightly in the sling.

"What the hell happened?!" the officer shouted.

"It got loose, tried to kill me," Taylor said innocently.

"Bullshit!! It was secured, I secured it!"

"Then *you'll* need to explain to Commander Keeb why this valuable *tech* got loose and had to be destroyed," Taylor said. "Now lower your rifles unless you want to explain why I was shot too."

Rifle muzzles lowered, but their expressions of disbelief remained.

"Sir--"

"Unfortunately, gentlemen, I need to see Commander Keeb immediately about this, it's very high priority. Excuse me," he pushed past them. Right now nothing would stop him from leaving, even if he didn't know where he was going. He just knew he had to walk. John was finally at rest. Taylor could see in his robotic eyes that he needed it to end. But the real John, the man who killed his own family to spare them from Jack Sethren, the real John's vengeance remained incomplete. That burned like the sun.

He cursed himself as he approached his old place a half an hour later. Taylor had fumed about it all the way to the home he once shared with Vina. He didn't ask himself why he went there. He was alone, confused, angry, and he went to her. If he thought about it for a moment, he would have stopped himself. She didn't need his poison anymore. Vina must have seen him coming, she walked out of the doorway before he had a chance to knock.

"Taylor. I told you once, you can't come here," Vina said.

"Vin, just listen to me, just for a minute," Taylor started. If she gave him the chance, he could have apologized to her, for everything.

"For the last time...shit, Taylor, your arm...your face...are you alright?" Her eyes changed, her wall was gone, she was worried about him.

And then Taylor's self loathing came back. He couldn't do it to her. Vina was going to give in, to melt, to take care of him despite the things he had put her through. Hell, that's why he came here, for her compassion. He wanted her compassion. But he wasn't going to do that to her. He had hurt her enough.

He was shaking.

"Are you okay, Taylor?"

"Fuckin' fine," Taylor said as he walked away. He left Vina on her porch, staring after him, with a confused expression on her face. He was sparing her the emotional energy she was about to waste on him. For the first time he wished things were the way they used to be.

Taylor fumed about it all the way to Catheri's place.

Taylor rounded the corner to her house, but beyond that he was lost. He didn't know why he was here. He was still angry, scared, and alone, and didn't know where to go. He was shaken by everything that had happened, something he would have otherwise thought impossible. He was forced to admit that his experience with John touched him, in more ways than one. He was angry about his arm, angry being an understatement. Taylor didn't want to think about it, about anything. Before knocking on Catheri's front door, it popped open. Jaek stood in the doorway. Jaek held the blaster he had stolen from him.

"Jaek, how's things?" Taylor asked, almost rolling

his eyes.

"You need to stay away from my mom," Jaek said, Ayne's blaster held loose at his side. He was bouncing it off his leg nervously in small, imperceptible motions. Taylor could smell the adrenaline flowing through the punk kid.

"She's a big girl, she can make her own choices."

"So can I!" Jaek shouted.

Taylor was surprised the kid had it in him. "Look, if I'm such a bad guy, just shoot me already," Taylor said.

"I'm warning you!" Jaek said, thrusting the blaster at him.

Stupid kid. "Probably won't fire anyway, damn Asian blasters have poor circuitry," Taylor said. But the look in Jaek's eye told Taylor everything he needed to know. He *would* fire. It didn't matter if the gun was faulty or not. Jaek was ready to kill him. How did it come to this? Jaek was ready to *kill* him. Taylor didn't mind ruining Catheri's life, she was a big girl who made her own choices. But Jaek was about to ruin his own life, he was just a punk kid.

"Have it your way, kid," Taylor said. He couldn't blame Jaek as he walked away, Jaek was only doing what he thought was right. Taylor wished he had something like that, something worth ruining his life for. Taylor ruined his life all the time, but it was always for nothing. All he had now was this case he was working on, and it was too much for him.

Catheri opened her door to find Jaek covered in sweat staring blankly at the family view screen, watching the news of all things. His eyes were fixed, he wasn't really watching the news at all. When Jaek looked up he practically jumped, tucking his hands behind his back and walking to his bedroom.

"Hey?" she asked him.

"Just a sec, mom," Jaek shot back as he closed his bedroom door. He was hiding something behind his back, but Catheri didn't really want to know what it was. Probably a picture of a naked woman, he was at that age. She didn't need to traumatize him for life. She decided to change the subject and pretend not to notice.

"Has Taylor called?" she hollered as she dropped groceries on the counter. Baker breads, cheeses, a much finer wine than she usually afforded, and Taylor's favorite seafood mix of shellfish and octopus. With butter, herbs, and some sizzling on the fry pan Catheri was going to make a dinner that made up for the week he was having. Too bad such a meal cost her being late on her utilities bill. But Taylor was worth it. If she could afford his prosthetic replacement she would do that too, but that would come in time. Jaek reappeared looking like he just wiped his face down with a towel and brushed his hair.

"What did you say?" he asked looking elsewhere.

"I said has Taylor called? I was expecting him over sometime today," she repeated.

"Nope," Jaek said looking down at his shoes.

"Are you alright?" she asked and walked over to him. She placed the back of her hand against his forehead and then felt along his neck.

"I'm fine mom! He never comes over half the time anyway, why waste your time?" he argued to get away. He hated being mothered.

"Tonight he's coming over for sure. I just know it ... well never mind. I'll be in the shower, get me if he calls okay?" she asked suddenly running away to prepare herself.

"Sure mom," Jaek punched the wall as soon as she disappeared behind the bathroom door.

Taylor was in a bar. He had been drinking.
He did not intend to quit.

Ever.

"notha' one, bar man," Taylor slurred.

"Maybe you've had enough for one night, eh?" the
bartender asked.

"I'm a Detectif, kay? I *earned* that, kay?" Taylor
said through half opened eyes.

"Yeah. Sure then," the barkeeper poured another
despite the pain of watching Taylor continue. The price of
drinks may as well double from here on out. At least to pay
for the cleanup when they drag him away.

"I'm detectif," Taylor slurred again. "I *earned* that."

Taylor turned in his seat, eyes closed and arm resting
along the bar. The room spun, it was best not to close his
eyes after all. He needed another drink. He opened half an
eyelid and looked across the room at a busty young girl
talking to some guy across the table from her. She looked
over at Taylor and then back at her boyfriend. Taylor
slurred and leaned forward, closing his eyes. In a minute he
would go over there and show her what a real man was, not
like that punk she was talking to. Today was her lucky day.
Women loved a man with one arm who could hold his
liquor. He just needed a minute before he walked over there.

Chapter 21

Morning always came. His right arm was throbbing, which meant he needed more pain meds. Also, something was licking his face. It was rough, dry, and felt like a nail file. It had to be a cat. Definitely not soothing and encouraging like a dog's tongue, all warm and soft. That kind of comfort didn't find a man like Taylor. Taylor might have known a cat would lick him awake, and leave an exclamatory swath of irritated skin on his face. Such was his life, always cat tongue, never dog tongue. The cat smelled like a stray too. Still he refused to open his eyes. The world could wait. The raw, fresh air told him he was outside, with sounds of the city to match. What part of town was this? Taylor pushed the cat away and regretted it instantly. Everyone knew the best way to make a cat love you, try to get rid of it.

"Get away...ohhh....I said *get*," Taylor whispered. His headache wouldn't forgive him for raising his voice. He opened his eyes, there was a rusted green dumpster in front of him at an angle. No, he was the one at an angle. He rubbed his eyes and waited for his vision to sharpen. The cat nudged its head into his ankle. Taylor looked at the cat, a vendetta burning into his consciousness. How dare that fur ball wake him up. Taylor found the resolve to stand, with only a wobble or two, and promptly undid his pants. He released one of the most rancid pisses he ever had, and sent the cat scurrying and wet.

"This is my territory now, kitty kitty. Ohhh....," Taylor would never drink again. He really meant it. It took Taylor a few minutes of arguing with reality before he thought about moving on. When Taylor was finally ready, he walked to the end of the alleyway and tried to figure out which street was nearby. The sun was way too hot. He saw a sign that said Jackson St, but it wasn't a part he recognized yet. From the entrance of the alleyway he could see a quaint outdoor bistro across the street. There was a pitcher of water on an outdoor table, and it was more beautiful than a three breasted Brazilian woman. He crossed the street and claimed the table, helping himself to the pitcher, bypassing any need for a cup. After a series of loud gulps that garnered several disapproving stares, Taylor slammed the pitcher down and caught his breath. This was more than a hangover. Taylor realized food might help soak up some of the poison in his stomach, so he checked his pockets just to make sure he still had a wallet. He found it, wrapped in a pair of lace panties. He dropped them on the table and held his head. He couldn't remember who they belonged to.

Taylor shielded his eyes from the sun, contemplating if moving his chair away from the bright light would be worth the exertion of moving. His existence right now was an unkind one, self induced. A waiter finally arrived with a new pitcher of water and poured him a glass. Taylor snatched it before he was even done pouring and gulped it down. The waiter poured two more glasses before leaving and retreated to the far side of the bistro. With water dangling from his chin he opened the menu and picked the first neutral dish he saw, a bagel. His stomach turned. On second thought, water was fine after all.

A few memories surfaced from the night before in bits at a time. Taylor's clothes were soiled and wrinkled, and ripe with the scent of booze, woman, and sweat. He was surprised the waiter didn't tell him to shove off.

"Sir?"

Taylor squinted up at the scolding rays of light where a shadowy silhouette waited. It was the waiter holding a telecom.

"I'm sorry, but he said it's an emergency," the waiter said handing it to Taylor. He was almost afraid to see who this was.

"You are hard to find, but I see you survived,"

Persona's voice came through the speaker.

"Is there a tracking bug in my ass?"

"No, nothing that simple. I monitored street surveillance, compared facial data and known speech recognition patterns," he went on until Taylor cut him short.

"Can't you make it quick?" Taylor held his head and closed his eyes. Why, oh why, did he drink so much.

"You actually talked to John, I'd say that is fortunate for us. It saves us the effort of trying to explain everything."

"You haven't explained anything. Get to the point, I'm busy," Taylor said. The light was too bright.

"There isn't much time, but ironically, timing is everything. We have a small window to kill someone today," Persona said.

"Oh yeah, sure, why not. It's not a complete morning without killing someone. Who are we killing?" Taylor yawned.

"Today we kill Jack Sethren."

Taylor spit out his water. "Come again??"

"He will be in the Sethren Tower lobby at 1:15 pm. Forgive the short notice but this information was not easy to confirm. Be there. Take your blaster this time, we won't get an easier shot."

"Some plan," Taylor sighed, looking around as if he were already caught. One did not speak casually about murdering New Seattle City's finest Citizen. Taylor turned his head as a breaking news clip blared from a television inside the bistro, Taylor saw his own handsome face onscreen. Yep, busted already. Taylor watched from a distance, wondering what in the world could he possibly be seeing right now. The news clip named him as a person of interest in the recent spate of murders. There was even a reward for information leading to his arrest. Taylor subconsciously ducked his head down a little. It was time to go already. He dropped some cash on the table and walked away. The waiter called after him, until he saw how much cash lay on the table. Taylor didn't have it in him to run.

Taylor's head was swirling well before he saw himself on the news as a suspect in several murders. Was Keeb retaliating for blowing up John? No, or at least, not likely. Keeb wouldn't concoct something as widespread as this. Would he? Taylor's head hurt, trying to think. Keeb could be a suspect, why not. But if it wasn't Keeb, then this crazy accusation came from somewhere higher. It had to be from the same person who had been pulling his strings all along, if that paranoid theory were true, which Taylor still wasn't sure about. His mysterious puppeteer, Jack Sethren. Funny, he had a date to kill the man today.

He also had possibly the worst plan ever, to just walk up and shoot. Was Persona not concerned about Taylor's well being? Maybe there was also an escape route he didn't know about, hopefully. Not that Taylor was convinced he was going to do it in the first place. He did not commit murder because someone told him to. After talking to John, Taylor agreed wholeheartedly that Jack Sethren deserved to die. But Taylor had his own questions too. That's why he was going to Sethren Tower. Not because Persona told him to, though that might happen as well. He was going because all of his questions would receive no answers if he were arrested first. Persona was right about one thing, this was his window of opportunity. He had an hour to get there, which would be fine if he could go straight there. Now Taylor had to dodge every cop and keep his head low.

He followed streets and routes that he knew cops avoided, which meant alleyway after alleyway. The first one had a man who was likely dead laying facedown near a dumpster. Taylor wondered if that's how he looked this morning before the cat woke him up. Taylor kept walking, there were bad people in the dark alleys of this city. A little later he walked past a group of three men, thick jackets, neck tattoos, faces covered with ski masks. They looked ready to run across the street and rob someone or some place, and were quite shocked to see Taylor strolling by. Shocked enough that he walked in peace, most people knew not to mess with crazy. Taylor kept going. He wasn't trying to, but any time he looked up, he could see part of Sethren Tower. That must have been a part of Jack Sethren's plan, build a big tower and rub it in Taylor's face just to piss him off. Taylor stopped before exiting the next alleyway, examining the street from a distance. This was a busy road that led to Precinct Four, and he easily could be spotted here if he wasn't careful. As he waited he heard a small giggle, and then a heavy laugh. A girl in a short, torn purple skirt was dragging a man into the alleyway. They both looked shocked for a moment to see Taylor, but sensing her customer getting nervous the girl pulled him against the wall and lifted her skirt up. She wasn't about to miss out on this paycheck, whether or not Taylor was standing there. When the sounds of heavy grunts and pretend moans were too much for him, Taylor crossed the street with his head down. The City had such a clean face, but nobody wanted to look at what was underneath.

Taylor kept his head low to remain unnoticed as he crossed street after street. He was almost there, almost at Sethren Tower. He wasn't sure what he was about to do. He needed more information, and he eyed a couple of people on their private phones, wondering if he should steal one and try to contact Persona again. Something about plotting a crime made Taylor laugh. Was this really his life? When he didn't give a shit about anything, he was a shiny new Detective. When he actually tried to do something noble or good, he became a criminal? It was enough to make a man think, except Taylor, he was too hung over to contemplate it further.

It didn't take as long as Taylor had originally thought. Taylor made his entrance to the lower mezzanine and peered up at the great Sethren Tower. Staring at it, thinking about it, he just couldn't imagine that Jack Sethren was his father. It felt like a fantasy, a delusion every orphan would make, that the city's most important man was secretly their father. But it did explain a few things, if it were true. Things like his promotion, like Commander Keeb never actually punishing Taylor, no matter what he did. And then there was John, before Taylor ended him, saying that he hurt Taylor to hurt Jack Sethren. What else could that mean? Nothing in Taylor's experience prepared him for this situation as he paused long and hard, staring at the tower that defined New Seattle City. It *would* be nice to inherit that. Taylor would order the hot receptionist to bring him coffee every day, naked. Could Jack Sethren really be his father? Taylor knew the better question, what did it matter? It didn't. Jack Sethren was scum, and he deserved to die for what happened to the real John.

Taylor approached Sethren Tower, the gaping door-less entrance was waiting for him. Taylor had his blaster all morning, but it suddenly weighed a ton sitting in its holster. The time was 1:10 pm. What was he going to do? Kill Jack Sethren? Then what? Run for his life? Taylor still had too many questions. How would he answer them if he killed Jack Sethren? But if Persona was right, was this his only chance? Taylor couldn't decide, so he walked in, soiled, tired, one armed, and reeking of two day old clothes. He remembered the inside lobby, and he sat down in a plush chair between two large ferns. He could at least rest a moment. Hopefully a decision would come to him. He knew he wasn't ready to kill Jack Sethren, plain and simple. But he might not have a chance later, when he was ready. The blaster was aggravatingly chaffing the inside of his armpit now. Men in business suits avoided looking at him as Taylor surveyed the room, pretending to read a magazine with his one arm. He resorted to folding the magazine in half and reading whatever page it landed on. 1:12 pm. How did Persona know where Jack would be?

The receptionist saw him, it was just a sideways glance as she was busy speaking to a tall man in a brand new suit. Taylor wished she hadn't seen him. Taylor also wished he knew what this magazine was about. 1:15 pm.

Mr. Jack Sethren emerged from the elevator to his awaiting businessmen. They accordingly worked their handshakes and fake smiles. Right on time. This was it.

Taylor thumbed the blaster under his shirt. Was he really going to just walk up and shoot the guy? He rose and walked towards Jack, his hand not far from the gun. He had never killed anyone like this. He took another step towards him, taking a deep breath. He had never met Jack Sethren in person, he was bigger than he looked in the pictures. Taylor let his hand fall from the blaster. Looking at Jack Sethren, here and now, he knew. He couldn't do it. He couldn't kill the man without at least talking to him first, at least asking why. He had to know, absolutely had to, no matter how much he hated him.

"Dad!" Taylor called out. Okay, so he couldn't kill him. But he at least had to do *something*.

Jack Sethren looked across the lobby at Taylor, and with two words made everyone in the lobby silent. "Excuse me," Jack said.

Everyone's attention turned to Taylor.

"*Taylor*... "

"IIi. Sorry I missed Christmas dinner?"

Jack Sethren released a very long, controlled breath through his teeth before talking. "Taylor, we should talk in my office."

"Want to catch up on old times?" Taylor asked, struggling to keep from shaking. Maybe he could do it. What was he expecting, an apology? Kill the bastard. Just grab and shoot. Jack Sethren was right there, just like Persona said he would be. But… he couldn't, not like this.

"We will need some privacy," Jack said, glaring.

"Sure *dad*, anything for you, *dad*," Taylor said. Jack Sethren motioned to one of the elevators. Taylor kept a wary eye on Jack as he went to it. It wasn't too late to kill him. Maybe it would be easier upstairs, without a dozen witnesses.

As Taylor entered the elevator Jack unclenched his fists. Jack never showed an emotion that he didn't want to show, but with Taylor he had almost lost it. And telling the partners that he was his son? Taylor would pay for that dearly.

"Hey *dad*, which floor is your office? Wait! Top floor, right? Meet you there," Taylor smiled pressing a button and shutting the elevator. No one uttered a sound as Taylor's elevator ascended, on its way to the top floor. Jack Sethren leaned over to the receptionist behind the counter and whispered to her. She stood to address the group.

"Gentlemen, Mr. Sethren will unfortunately have to reschedule for tomorrow. We appreciate your understanding," she recited as Jack Sethren disappeared in the next waiting elevator.

Jack Sethren waited for the doors to close before he considered what to do next. He had to keep his anger in check, it would do little except cloud his judgment. If today was the day he had waited over three decades for, it was still too soon. All of his carefully laid plans were bearing their fruit, but today seemed too soon. Well, what choice did Jack have? In spite of all the setbacks his plan actually did work. Taylor had followed the breadcrumbs all the way here just like Jack wanted, despite the rogue help he was receiving, despite Keeb's incompetence. His plan ultimately worked, albeit sooner than Jack wanted, but it was too late to change that now. So be it, today would be the day. His concern now was making sure he could savor every moment of it. A thirty year plan. Only moments remained.

Taylor was the last clone, and Jack Sethren had looked forward to this moment every day. He rocked on his tiptoes waiting for the elevator to take him to the top of

Sethren Tower like a child with candy. He knew Taylor's reason for coming, it was to kill him. Regardless, his security detail would have to be dismissed, this could only be done alone. His guards were a redundant security anyways, Jack Sethren could more than handle himself. Hard to believe that it would all be over soon. Somehow that almost saddened him.

He paged his security chief.

"Clear the top three floors, disable all cameras immediately."

"Yes sir!" the operator sounded off. The moment would still be captured. Jack had his own personal camera that wasn't attached to internal security, it would document this event for him to replay over and over. He started pacing in the elevator, focusing on what he was about to do next. He punched the wall. Jack was more of a man than his dad *ever* was.

Sethren Tower was Jack's legacy that the world would remember. But if the world found out about Taylor or the others, his legacy would become infamy. Just the thought of it made his heart race. The elevator opened on the top floor, Jack Sethren entered his room, his footsteps echoing off the marble tiles. Taylor was there, waiting for him.

No…this wasn't for the world to know. This was just for him.

||Chapter 22||

"Nice place dad, very nice stuff," Taylor said, leaning against a marble pillar. *Pathetic*. Taylor had it all wrong, he always did. Jack Sethren was not Taylor's father.

"Do you recognize me?" Jack Sethren asked, biting his teeth. He had to hide his inner monster just long enough, reminding himself over and over. He wouldn't give Taylor, his father, the man who forged the monster Jack Sethren was today, the satisfaction of dying ignorant. His father had to suffer defeat at the hands of his *incompetent*, *incapable* son. A son who now ruled all of New Seattle City! That's right, the incompetent son now ruled the city. No, Jack Sethren owned the city! While his pathetic, drunk, detective dad could barely make it to work sober.

Taylor's eyes drooped down low and serious. His sarcastic facade melted away, years of unresolved turmoil surfaced on his face. No doubt he was thinking of the orphanage and blaming Jack for it. He deserved every day there and more! Jack could barely keep from killing him right now. Taylor knew *nothing* of misery.

"Is all of this good enough for you, father?" Jack Sethren asked, motioning to the view outside the tower.

"How's that?" Taylor asked.

What did Jack Sethren say?

Why was he calling Taylor *father*?

Jack noticed the confused look on Taylor's face. *Fool!* But it was impressive how Taylor had become so close to the real thing. He was even a pathetic married detective banging his secretary. Taylor remained silent. Perhaps Taylor *still* didn't understand.

"Taylor, *I'm* not *your* dad," Jack Sethren said.

He was telling the truth. Taylor knew a lie when he heard it. And it sent Taylor's head spinning. What was happening here? Jack Sethren wasn't his father... fine. But beyond that, Taylor couldn't connect the dots. He had something to do with Jack Sethren, didn't he? This was wrong in a way Taylor couldn't have anticipated, and he sensed his opportunity closing. If he was going to have a chance to kill Jack Sethren, he had to take it right now. Taylor swallowed his questions. "Well whoever you are, you're the last one on John's list. And I hate to see a job left undone," Taylor said. Like a blur Taylor reached, quick drawing his blaster. He aimed it center mass.

Jack Sethren moved so fast Taylor didn't have time to react. He brandished a blaster of his own and fired before Taylor could, the round actually ricocheted off Taylor's weapon. Taylor dropped the searing hunk of metal and nursed his burnt fingers. Jack actually shot the blaster out of Taylor's hand. No one could make that shot. Jack aimed again.

"Was *that* good enough for you, dad?!" Jack Sethren taunted.

Taylor dove to safety behind the marble pillar inside Jack's room, bracing as he waited for marble to explode behind him. Instead he heard only footsteps walking across the room. Jack uttered a command and all the lights in the room went out. Jack called him dad? Why?

Everything was dark, even the windows went black. The only light came from a closet across the room that Jack disappeared into. It took a moment but Taylor worked up the courage to come out from behind the marble pillar. It seemed Jack was expecting him to follow.

Taylor made his way through the dark around silhouettes of marble pillars. The light came from a hidden room. He approached slowly, wondering if Jack was about to spring out from behind the wall. This had to be a trap. Jack Sethren could have killed him, but instead he only disarmed Taylor. What was he waiting for? Taylor didn't want to follow, but it was too dark to make his way back to the elevator. And at this point, it was probably locked out even if he could.

"Do you like it? I made it myself. *You* said I would never make anything," Jack's voice echoed. Through the trap doorway Taylor could see Jack standing openly in the center of his hidden room. It was a storage room, completely hidden behind the main wall. A room Taylor would never believe existed. It had to be *seen* to be believed.

The room was a freezer, like the inside of a commercial freezer. Light stemmed from everywhere. There was nothing in the room except for Jack Sethren. The walls and ceiling and floor were all ice. Taylor looked closer at one of the walls to get a better look at something stuck inside the ice. He saw a hand. He looked down and saw a leg. Frozen in the ceiling above him was part of a man's torso.

Taylor covered his mouth, in all four directions bodies and limbs were contorted and frozen in the walls. Even the floor beneath him was strewn with frozen limbs. Taylor stood very still when he looked down at his feet. In the ice beneath him was a severed head, face preserved in its final moment of agony. It was looking up at him through the floor. Taylor saw this face everyday when he shaved in the mirror. It was *Taylor's* face.

"What do you think of me now, father?" Jack Sethren asked, beaming with pride. "You said I would never accomplish anything. What do you say now?" Jack's voice had an altogether different tone than before.

Taylor could not speak.

"Answer me!!" Jack shouted. Tears began streaming down his face, he batted at them with an angry hand. Taylor felt an anvil shaped pit sink deep in his stomach. Every face he saw was *his*, and there were dozens frozen in the ceiling, floor, and walls. It was his hair, his feet, and his hands. These were clones of *Taylor*. Jack Sethren kept a horror cave full of mutilated *Taylor* clones. And Jack was calling *him* dad.

Taylor had been mistaken, he was not Jack Sethren's son. He was something else entirely. What the hell? What did this mean, was he a clone of Jack Sethren's dad? Seriously?? He had to act, to say something. Anything. "I'm... I was wrong... I'm proud... of you... son," Taylor said stumbling through pauses. If he was to survive this he would have to gain the upper hand. And he would have to do better than that. Jack appeared surprised for a moment, but the look in his face returned.

"I don't *need* your pride," Jack's voice cracked as he screamed at Taylor. He did not resemble the great and powerful Jack Sethren. He looked more like a teenager, like Jaek did earlier that day, angry and insecure. This was beyond anything Taylor could have imagined. Jack aimed his gun, pointing it low.

"I've killed you a hundred times, but your death will never taste as sweet as this!!"

"Wait!!" Taylor shouted. Jack Sethren fired deliberately low with a shot that grazed Taylor's leg. He wasn't going to kill him with a single round. He was going to pick him apart and savor this kill. Taylor looked down where the round had kissed flesh, sensing his mortality. This was it. There was no escape. Taylor had walked straight to his death, and he was helpless to stop it. Taylor stared at his feet for a second. Well, if that's how it was, then so be it. Taylor wasn't going down quietly. He looked up.

"You little shit, you never did learn how to aim! You shoot like a girl! Did I raise a boy or a girl?? I can't tell from here," Taylor scolded. Jack's face went white. There were many things in Taylor's life that he had come to yell, cry, and throw a fit about at Jack Sethren, mostly regarding his childhood in the orphanage. They all disappeared, this was better. Jack Sethren was shaking like a five year old who just had his birthday taken away.

The lights went out, the room turned pitch black.

"Lights!" Jack shouted, firing a shot and missing wildly. "I said lights!! LIGHTS!!!"

Taylor ducked low and stumbled back to the trap door between this room and the marble palace. A chunk of wall blasted away as Taylor ducked out, particles flew into his hair and down his shirt. Taylor could see inside the elevator doors at the end of the marble tiled room. The doors had opened of their own accord. Taylor heard Jack Sethren right behind him.

"Lights damn you!!" Jack shrieked.

Jack's frustrated cries followed Taylor through the dark. Someone was helping Taylor escape, he knew because small lights flickered on the floor towards the elevator, dim and brief, meant for Taylor's eyes only. The elevator itself was just slightly illuminated, just enough to keep Taylor from running into the wall. Persona was doing this. Taylor jumped in the open elevator and pressed his body against the side wall as Jack Sethren screamed after him like a man possessed. The doors closed, and not a second later Taylor jumped when Jack's fists pounded on the outside. Thankfully the elevator instantly whisked Taylor upwards. Why up?

This was not good. He should have killed Jack in the lobby. A vision of the severed head in ice made him double over and vomit. The more he tried to shut those images out of his head the more they fought back. Taylor pieces, frozen for all time in Jack Sethren's personal freezer. Taylor paced back and forth in the elevator. He had to get out of here before he lost his mind. The elevator opened to the roof where a powerful chill swept across. The air was cold today. The clouds were angry.

"Hurry Taylor! Jack is right behind you," Persona's voice spoke through a speaker in the elevator. "Go!!"

"GO WHERE?!" Taylor shouted back. Taylor stumbled away from the elevator. "WHERE?!"

The world sprawled beneath him from the top of Sethren Tower. It was as if he could see the Earth's curve, swallowed by a distant quilt of clouds. City streets lay at his feet. He could see mountain ranges fifty miles away, maybe farther. He saw the lawless wastelands beyond the city, endless green forests, inlets of vast ocean from the harbor, all very spectacular if he wasn't about to be murdered.

The elevator doors reopened.

Jack Sethren burst from the elevator, his head whipped left and right searching for Taylor, teeth glistening even on this cloudy afternoon. He swung the blaster back and forth, furious and desperate. There was nowhere to hide up on top of Sethren Tower. Taylor could not die at this madman's hands, too many had already. He stood near the edge. Taylor did not look down. He had mustered the resolve to die moments before Persona tried to help him escape. At least Taylor could rob Jack Sethren of the moment he had waited so long for. Jack Sethren saw Taylor and aimed the blaster at him. Taylor turned to jump.

"NO!!" Jack Sethren cried, aiming and firing without precision.

For a moment there was no such thing as gravity, only air, rushing by and then faster and faster. Taylor looked up at the clouds as he fell. They blurred from the wind rushing by. Tears streaked past his face. Taylor closed his eyes. At least he chose this.

So much air rushing past him made it hard to breath, the top of the tower was barely visible now. He thought of Vina, he was happy she was moving on.

Taylor could hear the a-grav lightrails as if they were hovering next to him. He opened his eyes when he realized how that was impossible. A blurry winged flyer was matching his rate of descent. Before Taylor had a chance to react it swooped underneath him, cradling him with the dexterity of an acrobat, and flew him away from the rushing ground below.

Taylor gasped, breathing in and out in uncontrolled

bursts. He held onto the flyer with all the strength of a desperate man. He had embraced death, but now he had the chance to live. It was a hope he was afraid to give in to, for all he knew this was Jack Sethren's mini flyer bringing him right back.

The flyer streamed through the sky with comforting dexterity, Taylor held on but was able to do so easily. The flyer adapted easily to wind and air. It toured the city over Pike's Place market and dodged between various sky scrapers until it landed on a nondescript building on the far side of the harbor. The flyer landed gracefully as a heron, rolling softly to a stop.

Taylor stood atop an apartment building, old and the very definition of inconspicuous. Taylor walked away from the flyer towards an entry door dangling on bent hinges. Inside he saw a gaping rotating platform where an elevator shaft used to be. He jumped onto the roving platform as it cycled its way down and then hopped off onto the only open floor available. Inside was a room. Felix's face, the very same man who killed himself on Fifth Ave, right in front of Taylor, was looking back at him from a holoscreen placed in the center of the studio.

"We'll need a new plan now, Taylor."

]]Chapter 23[[

Taylor collapsed to the floor. In his lifetime he had been tazed and phased and many other manner of incapacitation. Jack Sethren, naturally, had something beyond all of that. He had the purely cerebral truth that Taylor was a clone built for no purpose beyond Jack's enjoyment to torture and kill. It was enough to incapacitate Taylor. Even after having leapt to death from the top of Sethren Tower, the truth is what turned him inside out. He leaned against the wall near the rotating elevator unit and just rested.

The room was dominated by a large holoscreen. Surrounding it were shelving units, workbenches, and hundreds of automated server bots. More *tech* existed in this room, in a building that city planners probably were planning to demolish, than anywhere he had ever seen or heard of. Felix was onscreen, except now Taylor realized it was actually Persona. This was where Persona was hardwired to the rest of the world, this was his mainframe. He looked exactly like Felix did.

The workbench on the far wall was blanketed with moving tools and robotic arms like an assembly line. Small tools operated independently next to the mechanical arms, assembling various projects that Taylor couldn't identify. Computer towers lined the opposite wall, powerful refrigeration units built beneath and above, network cables thick as Taylor's neck dangled and stretched across the room. Taylor suspected this was Persona's home. Felix really was clever.

All of Taylor's life had been spent with a buried anger for the life he endured. Only now he knew it wasn't a random thing or just bad luck. His turmoil had actually been planned. It didn't make him mad, it was actually liberating. He really sort of thought life was just out to get him. Now he knew it wasn't his fault, any of it. It was the best news he had all week. His life sucked, because of someone else, not because he deserved it. It really felt great to know that now. Persona had been speaking to him.

"A body didn't hit the ground, Taylor. Jack Sethren will come for you, there is nowhere safe from him. Not even here."

"Doesn't matter," Taylor said, "I'm done. I don't care anymore."

"This is new territory for both of us. Hear me out," said Persona. "Then you can decide."

His assistant walked in, shaking, terrified. He did not want to be the one who approached Jack Sethren right now. "Mr. Sethren, I have good news," he trembled.

"GET OUT OF HERE!!" Jack screamed. He stood among the scattered remains of his once beautiful marble palace.

"He never hit the ground, there wasn't a body," the guard reported before fleeing the room.

Jack Sethren paused. He held a piece of marble in his hand, one of thousands decorating the floor now. Did Taylor live? Please, oh please let him still live!! The marble shattered into dust as he squeezed. He would call Commander Keeb immediately. He would order a full scale man-hunt, but with the discreet instruction of bringing Taylor here, alive, unharmed. Keeb would have to see to it personally. He wanted every officer wearing a badge roaming the streets for Taylor. Nowhere was safe to hide from Jack Sethren!

"I didn't realize how handsome I looked onscreen," Taylor said, admiring himself as he watched his face on the news. Apparently there was a manhunt for Taylor, every badge in the city was looking for him. The moment he stepped outside he would be found. Taylor figured that meant he wasn't able to call himself a detective anymore.

"Yo, doc," Taylor called. Persona appeared back onscreen. "How long is this gonna' take?" Taylor asked.

"It's just now ready. Taylor, this will hurt. It's going into the bone."

"Just do it already."

A six wheeled mini crawler, like the ones used to explore Mars and the moon for resources, brought over the blue *'gel'* arm. Persona explained that it was going to replace his missing arm using some kind of response tech, the gel material would feel like skin. It was durable, lightweight, and interfaced easily with the human nervous system, not to mention computers. Persona said it was technology from the lost age.

"What do you have to do with any of this? Why do you care about John and his revenge?" Taylor asked, killing some time while he waited.

Persona rarely waited on answering. He didn't need time to think. "John was our friend and colleague. After living in denial for so long, we realized we couldn't ignore the guilt, especially after John, or the android of him, came back. We called it fate."

"So, you blew your brains out because you lived and the rest didn't?"

"I did not. Felix did. I am Persona. But we had spent our lives making Jack Sethren the people's champion. And we sold our friend's lives to do it."

"You made the devil a saint and wanted to wash your hands of sin," Taylor said.

"So it seems," Persona agreed. Taylor felt little metal arms wipe his skin down with alcohol, he watched to see the robots insert tiny painless needles in his skin, prepping for the gel arm attachment.

"Is this gonna---AHH!!" Taylor cried out as the service bot sliced open his skin and severed through bone. Taylor was frozen still, immobilized by an electrode needle in his neck from a second bot, a handy way to restrain someone, but with unbearable pain. Taylor's eyes swelled with pressure as every muscle in his body snapped taut. Little robotic hands pulled open flesh and bone. Taylor felt himself about to pass out, and then he suddenly jolted back awake. An arch of electricity soldered the new gel arm to his flesh. The moment the gel touched his skin it swarmed with sensations, sending responses through his nervous system. He felt a wave of sensory input, every artificial follicle bombarded his nervous system with responses. Then it roared back down, and the pain was all but dissipated, controlled by the gel arm's response system. Taylor closed his eyes, unable to ride the roller coaster of signals his body was processing. The gel arm seemed to rise and fall with sensation, as tiny receptors gauged feedback and stabilized their signal strengths. The pain was fully gone now, but the gel arm still felt swollen and tingly, slowly receding, finally getting to a place that didn't make Taylor hold his chair for fear of vomiting. As soon as it let him, Taylor was making a fist and flexing his artificial wrist. After another minute, it actually felt very good, almost normal, almost natural, and strong. *Very* strong. It looked like an arm made of murky blue gel.

"It will determine levels of pain through feedback in your nervous system. For example, if someone steps on your hand you will feel it. But if someone thrusts a knife through your hand, it won't really hurt. A form of controlled sensory response. They tried no pain, but the body accepts it better when it feels something. The swelling will go down soon, too."

"Don't ever do that again. If you do, I'll upload myself in there and kick your ass. Got it?" Taylor snarled. Having a new arm distracted him from whatever Persona said in retort. He wiggled his fingers again. It felt great. He never knew how much he would enjoy being roboman until he rubbed his hand through his hair, every bristle of hair could be felt through his gel fingers. His arm was better than new. "It's about damn time," Taylor said, admiring his arm. "So, how does the world find out about the bad side of Jack Sethren," Taylor asked.

"Maybe it doesn't," Persona replied.

"What? Then what is the plan?"

"Kill the devil, but save the saint. Jack *must* suffer, but New Seattle City should not."

"Look robo nut, I better make the plans from now on. The last one was crap," Taylor said, walking around the room slapping server bots and knick knacks with his gel arm. His arm felt incredible. "I say what goes around comes around," Taylor said as he punched a brick wall, the brick splintered beneath the force of his gel fist. *Wow*. He grabbed one of the serve bots and crushed it. "Oops."

Taylor had to wonder what Jack's real dad, Taylor's genetic original, was like in real life. What if Taylor was just like him? He must have at least looked like him. Jack Sethren's dad must have been a real bastard. Well, Taylor always knew he was a bastard too, but at least now it wasn't his fault.

"There's one more thing, Taylor. You had the chance to kill Jack Sethren, but you weren't sure. You have to be sure next time. You can't have any doubts over what we are about to," Persona said.

His voice was identical to a few moments ago where he told Taylor it might hurt a little. Taylor looked over at the screen, and then it hit him.

"What is that?" He felt something interacting with his brain, struggling to take over. Images, memories, flooded his mind, memories that were not his. Taylor instantly collapsed to the floor, rolling and fighting, kicking, convulsing. Whatever this was, it was attacking his brain directly. His nerves fought against the digital signals trying to take over, but he was helpless to stop it.

"I've stored John's memories in that gel arm. You need to see what you are fighting for."

Wave after wave of foreign thoughts surged into Taylor, he had no control over them. Then darkness. Suddenly Taylor was on a space station. Space Station Hephaestus, he knew its name. He saw John's children, only they felt like *his* children. He felt the fear of the Elites outside his door. He felt everything John felt and lived every fear and regret. He felt John rip out his heart, the moment he protected his family one last time. He was living John's last days.

"Stop!! Please stop!!" Taylor smashed his arm into the wall, trying to tear it off. Then it was over. Taylor lay on the floor convulsing from the residual aftereffects. They were his memories now. When the range of sensations subsided, when he could differentiate between John's memories and his own, he sat up.

What the arm showed him changed everything. There was no middle ground, no ounce of effort he would spare. All the while Persona looked on, an image of understanding in his binary interpretation of a brain. Taylor knew now what cargo lock five meant, and how it was John's tomb. He knew why John came back and killed, even though the real John died thirty long years ago. The memories were very real, and they were now his memories too. He was grateful, in a way. He had never known such emotions, a word that failed to describe the depths of what he just experienced. He knew his purpose. But how would he get to Jack Sethren again?

He knew what he couldn't do. He couldn't return to Precinct Four, he was no longer a detective. He couldn't walk the streets of his beloved city, not while Commander Keeb launched a full scale manhunt for him. Taylor could probably keep from getting shot during the arrest, but he would never be able to convince anyone of his innocence. But with what he knew now, it didn't matter what it would take. He had to finish this.

"Jack Sethren will not live to see another day," Taylor vowed.

But how to make it happen? Taylor had few resources available. Vina had left him. But Taylor didn't deserve her, and it brought him a sense of calm to know she was better off. Catheri loved him with all her heart, but thanks to Jaek he would not use her anymore. Now Catheri was better off too. He did at least have a purpose. He knew why he was put on this earth, twisted as it may be. Knowing these things gave him a stability he never had in life. And the inferno sparked within him from John's memories would rage on until Jack was dead. He knew he would *find* a way to Jack Sethren once more.

Taylor was glad he put the androids out of their misery, John had suffered enough and their existence was an abomination. Yet John's soul and the soul of his children deserved revenge, a revenge that Taylor would give his life for. He loved those children so much…and they were never his children. Taylor was awash with another man's worst moments in life.

"Persona, you really could have warned me first," Taylor said rubbing his arm.

"Next time I'll warn you better," Persona said. Taylor prayed there would not be any next time.

"Do you have a plan?" Persona asked.

"Jack Sethren needs to suffer," Taylor said. "But death is not enough. If there is a hell beyond death, the devil will only welcome Jack home. There has to be a way to make Jack Sethren feel the pain he caused John," Taylor said.

"Well, you are his father, sort of," Persona mused.

Taylor looked at Persona's face on the screen. "What are you thinking of?" Taylor asked.

Jack Sethren cleared the room for the third time. Even Kita was sent away. He cancelled his meeting with the businessmen, and even being Jack Sethren they would not tolerate that for long. His careful plans, his thirty years of waiting and waiting, were all ruined. Keeb's incompetence knew no boundary, Taylor would never be found. Taylor was an expert coward, and with his experience and resources, he was easily capable of disappearing. Having seen the truth, especially the freezer room, he would have every reason to disappear forever. Jack Sethren was ready to tear the city apart earlier. Slowly he realized it wouldn't help.

But even Jack Sethren didn't know everything. Just as his desperation was collapsing into rage, his telephone buzzed. It was a private line, no one had access to this number that Jack didn't personally trust. Yet he couldn't imagine who might try to reach him.

"What!?" Jack snapped into the phone.

"Jack, Taylor was found hiding in an abandoned warehouse. Officers placed him under arrest without incident," Keeb said in his usual monotone. Jack was almost afraid to believe it. "I'm bringing him to you now as ordered," Keeb said. Jack Sethren smiled from ear to ear. He overestimated Taylor. A mistake he was happy to make for once.

"Commander, I am impressed. You will be mayor one day! Drive to the receiving doors, lower basement entry, alone. I'll clear the floor of any witnesses."

"Half the precinct knows of his arrest," Keeb said.

"He was killed while trying to escape. Don't worry, I won't take long," Jack smiled. He was back in business.

"Kita!" Jack Sethren called.

"Mr. Sethren?" she answered right away over the speaker. Anything she could do to lessen Jack's temper was her highest priority.

"Clear the basement receiving levels three and four immediately. You have two minutes. And I will not be kind to anyone I find down there, is that clear?" he said.

"Right away sir," she replied. Jack paced for the two minutes he gave Kita, looking at the mess of his marble palace. It was due for a remodel anyway, green marble tiling had become stale. When he could wait no longer, Jack rushed to the elevator and slapped the basement button a dozen times. He almost never went to the lower levels of the tower. Taylor would be in restraints, Jack knew how he wanted to kill him. He would strangle him to death. Of all the ways he killed the other clones, strangling was the most deeply satisfying. There was a special connection with that manner of kill; the intimate look in their eyes, the despair as they knew the end was coming. And best, his hands could feel the life drain away, squeezing every last bit of it. He couldn't wait.

It was a pity that this would be the last time. He had invested the most effort in Taylor, the one clone who he grew from a baby to a man. Keeping tabs on him every step of the way, introducing people into his life that Jack carefully selected. He kept everyone from ever being kind to Taylor growing up. And the one person who befriended him, that teacher *Ms Payer*, he found a way to manipulate that too. She was genuinely kind to Taylor. Jack decided to let their bond grow so it hurt him the most when he killed her. And having her killed on Taylor's birthday... Jack couldn't have planned that any better. But Taylor was the last clone. This was the last chapter, after a lifetime of hatred it was time to close the book on his father. If such a book could be closed.

 The elevator went down, down, farther down than Jack Sethren could remember descending before. He was not certain he had ever been to the basement level of his own tower. It finally stopped and the doors opened. The cold concrete rich air of the City swarmed around him as the elevator doors receded. Jack Sethren scanned the basement level to make certain everyone was gone. Only a sole police Cruiser waited, as ordered. Taylor was inside, Jack could feel it.

 Jack Sethren approached the Cruiser, waiting to see Commander Keeb. The Cruiser door opened and Taylor stepped out, unaccompanied and unrestrained.

 "Commander Keeb?" Jack called out.

 "Oh, yeah. Sorry. Keeb said he was busy. I hope that's not a problem for you," Taylor said. Taylor looked far too confident to be under arrest. "He said I should just go down here, turn myself in. I'm trying to be good about following orders and all."

 "What the hell is this?"

 "This is the end of Jack Sethren. This is what you've got coming to you," Taylor said. He noticed Jack standing with his shoulder at Taylor slightly, a subtle change that made him less of a target.

 Jack Sethren smiled. "Keeb isn't here."

 "Nope," Taylor said.

 Jack nodded. "This was a clever way to get to me, perhaps the only way," Jack said. Anger was finding its way into his eyes.

 "Thanks," Taylor said.

 Jack snarled. "Your victory will be short lived," Jack said as he pulled out his telecom to dial Kita.

 "Hello Jack," a male voice answered.

 Jack Sethren was stunned for a moment. "Felix?" Jack knew the voice well, yet Felix had been missing for weeks. It was Taylor who piped in.

"Yeah, no, I keep doing that too. It's not Felix, it's Persona. And he's really good at impressions. Wasn't that a great impression of Keeb? Even had me fooled," Taylor said.

"Get me security!!" Jack Sethren yelled at the basement cameras.

"Sorry Jack. Waving at the cameras won't help, I've taken care of that."

Jack Sethren bit the corner of his lip and then smiled. He looked at Taylor and dropped his phone. He was trapped, but they would learn what an animal does when trapped. Truth of it was, Jack Sethren was feared long before he had a tower and bodyguards to hide behind. He had come here to kill Taylor with his bare hands, and that was exactly what he was going to do.

"That's a nice arm you have, Taylor. *Gel*?" Jack Sethren asked. In a way, it concerned Taylor that Jack knew the technology and wasn't afraid of it. To make it worse, Jack could read Taylor's concern like a neon sign.

"I have a few modifications myself," Jack smiled. Taylor clenched his gel fist. Jack cracked his neck from ear to ear. Taylor and Jack stared each other down, waiting for one man to make the first move.

"I should have used birth control," Taylor said.

Jack Sethren moved like lightning, so fast Taylor lost sight of him. Jack disappeared behind one pillar and like a magician appeared from the next. It wasn't just fast, it was inhuman. Jack Sethren had modifications that superseded anything Taylor had ever seen, modifications that Persona had warned him about. Regardless, Taylor had a plan, more or less. Winning the fight wasn't the goal here, letting Jack get close was. Taylor didn't know what to expect next, when suddenly hands were clenched around his throat. Hands more powerful than Taylor would have imagined. His human hand struggled to pry the grip free but his gel hand ripped fingers loose just before his throat was crushed. Gasping for air Taylor spun to face Jack and took a kick in chest that sent him flying through the air.

The kick sent Taylor into the wall, luckily he broke his fall with the gel arm instead of his skull. Concrete cracked from impact. Taylor slumped against the wall using a hand to keep upright. He kept his head down and watched Jack Sethren approach from the corner of his eye. Sensing a downed opponent Jack strolled towards him. Jack just needed to step a little bit closer. Taylor's plan was to act hurt and let Jack Sethren get close. His plan was still working, the only change was that he didn't have to act at all. He was getting his ass totally kicked.

Taylor grabbed Jack's ankle and squeezed, springing to action.

"AGH!!" Jack recoiled in pain as Taylor crushed his ankle. Springing off the ground he picked Jack up like a fireman and slammed him against the wall. Jack brought his arms in and with a burst of strength pushed Taylor back so hard it flung him twenty meters. Taylor landed in a roll and scrambled to his feet. Jack looked to the far corner of the basement and in the next instant was gone.

"Damn it!" Taylor swore. He pulled out his left handed blaster, slipped the safety free and felt its circuitry warm in his hand. He listened for sounds of Jack Sethren. He heard something sneaking towards him, getting ready to pounce from across the parking garage.

Taylor waited, his timing had to be perfect. Jack Sethren appeared out of nowhere, coming hard with a fist meant to take Taylor's head off. Taylor raised his gel arm to block, Jack's punch hit so hard that a chunk of gel flew off. With a cry of determination Taylor charged, his hands leapt out and snatched Jack by the throat. He carried him three steps and slammed him against a support pillar.

Taylor had to be careful how hard he squeezed. He didn't want Jack to die yet. Jack Sethren gasped for air, a high pitched squeal that meant he was squeezing just enough. "Now!!" Taylor shouted, and his blue gel arm began to glow. Jack's eyes bulged as he watched a gel worm emerge from Taylor's arm. He struggled to break free, but Taylor squeezed him still. The finger thick mass inched across Taylor's arm, up his hand, and onto Jack's throat until finding the ear.

"NO!!" Jack shrieked. The worm inched itself through Jack's ear canal, Jack fought back in desperation but Taylor held him firm. When the worm fully inserted itself into Jack's brain his eyes rolled into the back of his head. He let go of Jack's throat and took a step back. Taylor knew what happened next. He experienced it himself, only Jack Sethren would not survive this. The gel worm that was connecting directly to Jack's brain would see to that.

"Rest in peace, John. You, and your family," Taylor said.

Everything that Persona had shown Taylor was going through Jack Sethren right now, all of it. He would suffer John's final days, the pain of poisoning his wife and children, the agony inside cargo lock five waiting to die, the disintegration of his sanity as he struggled to activate the androids. Jack Sethren would die suffering the pain he caused.

It was beautiful vengeance.

Taylor looked on as Jack Sethren's body heaved, for one last moment studying the man who created him. Soon the City would be wondering what happened to Jack Sethren. And the manhunt underway for Taylor would be tripled.

"Well Felix, what do you think we should do now?"

"I'm not Felix, I told you. And what do you mean, we? Jack Sethren is seconds away from death. Our partnership has no purpose now."

"I was thinking of renaming you. Persona is a stupid name. And why not *we*? I think *we* make a good team. Besides, I need your help with something else," Taylor said.

"What's that?"

"This. More of this. Purpose... I don't know. Jack Sethren wasn't the only piece of shit to walk the earth you know, and besides, you make a good partner tucked in my *gel* arm and all," Taylor said.

"You want to exact revenge for people who themselves cannot?"

"I was thinking of something more high class, like vigilantes," Taylor corrected him. Looking at the convulsing Jack Sethren, Taylor smiled. His life had finally just begun. Knowing everything about his beginning, about his horrible childhood and the life that followed, it made Taylor free, though he couldn't say how. But that couldn't be the end of it. He had waited his whole life for a purpose, for meaning to his existence. Now that he finally had that, he wasn't going to just let it go. Jack Sethren stared up at nothing, eyes and mouth wide open.

"Drink this sweetpea, everything will be fine in a minute," Jack Sethren said as Taylor was walking away. Taylor stopped. He tried not to remember it himself, but those words hit him. He wiped a tear from his eye before it could fall. It was John's memory, but it was Taylor's now too. He called his little girl 'sweetpea', even when he gave her that cup full of poisoned juice. It was a dignified death, a peaceful death, something he had to do. If there was any other way… he would have embraced it. Taylor started walking again. It didn't happen to him, but it may as well have. The memories were his now too.

Taylor knew what came next. Jack Sethren was living through John's final hell. And it was far from over.

The End

Other Titles by N.R. Burnette:
KENJI

KENJI is a fantasy novel of distant worlds and the gods that rule them. When Gojun, the god of war, is betrayed he vows to burn the gods and make the Fates return his murdered wife. To save themselves, the gods seek out Gojun's lost son, Kenji. Armed with his budding powers and a natural drive for war, Kenji is caught in a struggle against his sudden god destiny and his own love for a goddess.

PAPHOS (Complete Series)

Seven doomed explorers, trapped, hunted, and turned against one another. When Austin brought his daughter to the unexplored planet Paphos, it was supposed to be a chance to reconnect with her. But when he and his crew of scientists discover an alien facility, all of that changes...

Visit www.nrburnette.com **for more!**

Questions, comments, and feedback:
nrburnette@nrburnette.com

Follow me on:
http://twitter.com/nickburnette

Made in the USA
San Bernardino, CA
26 April 2014